Legends and Popular Tales of the Basque People

The Folk Stories, Myths and Ballads of the Basque Country

By Mariana Monteiro

With illustrations by Harold Copping

Published by Pantianos Classics

ISBN-13: 978-1-78987-148-7

First published in 1887

Contents

Introduction

ON placing before the reader this collection of Basque legends, fairy tales, ballads, and popular stories having their origin in the ancient traditions which formed a portion of the sacred inheritance bequeathed to the Basque people by their forefathers, and handed down by word of mouth from generation to generation; I have thought that a few remarks would not be out of place concerning the moral and historical importance which these legends and tales possess, as being the reflection of the ideas and faithful echo of the sentiments of past generations.

If at one time these legends were viewed with contempt by superficial minds that could not perceive behind the simplicity of their form the great lessons which they inculcated, and the lofty sentiments they enclosed, these very tales and legends are in our day becoming the objects of the attention and study of deep thinkers who, by the meagre light which these tales alone afford them, are able to penetrate the shadows left by those ancient societies that have disappeared from the face of the globe, carrying along with them the secrets of their ideas, civilization, and life, because these traditions constitute the archives of the people, the treasures of their science and of their beliefs; they are the records of the lives of their forefathers, the landmarks of the grandeur of their past history.

The Basques, like all primitive races, separated from the common paternal family, and holding similar beliefs and customs, must necessarily possess many analogous points in common, independent of the effects due to difference of climate, mode of living, religion, and other physical and moral causes. Yet the Basques are singular in this, that, in the midst of the great revolutions which have agitated the whole of Europe, causing radical changes, levelling to the ground or converting into ruins great empires, powerful nationalities, monuments; sweeping away languages, and even the very races themselves-- the Basques have known how to pass unscathed through the many storms of devastation, preserving intact their nationality, institutions, laws, language, and customs.

Impelled by their singularly energetic activity, and by the strength of their warlike spirit, they have fought on land, they have triumphed by sea, they have explored and conquered unknown regions; and, by the light of their unassuming but practical intelligence, have succeeded in consolidating with admirable harmony the elements of a wise rule which perhaps has no equal in the world. But following that traditional spirit which is the characteristic mark of the race, and trusting to that spirit for the preservation of their institutions and history, they have never sought to transmit in writing to their descendants the narrative of their great deeds, nor the keystone of their robust organization, nor, indeed, in one word, the secret of that immense sovereignty to which they attained, and which is scarcely comprehensible in our day if we take into account the now limited conditions of their territory and wealth.

What interest and importance must be attached to collecting, in view of all these circumstances, the thousands of scattered fragments of a nation's traditions and beliefs which, shining like vivid flashes of lightning amid dark shadows, rend the dense veils which conceal the mysterious secrets of the glorious history of the Basque people?

There are some who would fain put down all popular beliefs on the plea that they perpetuate superstition in the heart of the people. That the masses are superstitious is unfortunately a truth which cannot be denied; but, at the same time, it is true to say that the greatest men and the most illustrious people of the world have yielded to that weakness. Yet this fact does not prove that it is only in traditional beliefs where the origin of the evil is to be sought for. So long as we are unable to define the limits which separate truth from error in space and time, in the physical and moral worlds, man will ever allow himself to be carried away by the irresistible yearning for that which is unknown and incomprehensible, to seek in the mysterious regions of fancy for abundant food to satisfy his curiosity, and some explanation for that which he cannot understand.

By no other means is it comprehensible how superstition has always subsisted in every race, whatever be the religious profession or degree of culture it may have reached, or age in which it existed. The object may have changed, the form may have varied, as it has always done under the various influences exercised by religion, climate, customs, and other causes; nevertheless superstition has not ceased to pervade and dominate the spirit as powerfully now as it has ever done.

It is true that in our days the belief in witches is gone by, but, on the other hand, a world of spirits have risen up, or rather been discovered, as many spiritualists assert, who assume to live in perfect union with them.

We have among us mediums who have, so they tell us, legions of the dead at their command ever ready to appear at their evocation to fill with wonder and dread the most cultured city of Europe. And if all the world laughs at divination and the magic arts, there are few who do not shudder when some somnambulist, with brow bathed in perspiration and frame quivering in forced sleep, assures them that he can perceive through his closed eyelids the beginning of tubercule in the lungs of a patient, or some latent disease in the heart.

Ancient beliefs as a rule sprang from faith or some moral sentiment in such a manner that across their gross fictions there shone some great truth or deeply rooted virtue. Hence they always left behind some moral teaching or called forth some wholesome emotion. And in proof that the beliefs of our forefathers tended to inspire the noblest instincts in man, we have but to take any of the simplest of them. Who, for instance, has not heard hundreds of times in the Basque Provinces, in one form or another, the tales of the *Arguiduna*?

"The day has fled, and the poor cottager trudges sadly up the mountain path which leads to her house. She is weeping, her heart is torn asunder by grief, for she has lost her only child, who was the sunshine of her life.

"The shades of twilight, the silence which surrounds her, the sad mystery of night renew the wounds of her heart! She thinks of her child, she weeps, looks up to heaven and goes on her way!

"She proceeds, and reaches the graveyard where but a few days since she had laid the loved remains, and the poor mother on beholding the grave puts both her hands to her beating heart, feeling as though it must needs burst in twain under that wave of sorrow and bitterness which the recollection of her loss has raised.

"Suddenly a weird light, mysterious, leaps over the low wall of the cemetery and approaches to meet her, flickering in fantastic movements amid the shades. On beholding that light the mother falls on her knees, puts out her hands towards the flame, and, forgetful of her own pain, she asks in a faltering voice

"'Child of my heart, are you happy?'

"And the light, as though wishful of replying to her, becomes agitated and moves rapidly, and approaches nearer and closer to her, and stands still above her head. The woman, enraptured by an undefinable emotion, closes her eyes. Who knows? Perchance her ears have caught the sweet murmur of the words of her son--perchance she has felt on her lips the loving kiss of that idolized child of her heart!

"But the light begins to ascend and continues rising towards heaven until it becomes lost amid the shadows. The woman stands for a moment, her eyes fixed with fond looks on the spot where the light has vanished. She then directs to heaven a prayer, and starts on her way home, weeping still; but the tears she sheds are tears of resignation which comfort her. That night, sleep does not desert her eyelids as on previous nights, nor is she troubled by visions or phantoms. She sleeps calmly, awakes with peace of soul. And this is due to her having seen the spirit of her child; it is because she knows that the child so beloved and wept for has not forgotten his poor mother; it is that she feels that the soul of the child of her affections has gone to be reunited with its kindred spirits, the angels of heaven!"

What has all this been? If you question science it will tell you that it is due to a very simple phenomenon. Some gases emanating from the organic bodies of that graveyard have become inflamed on coming into contact with the air, and produced that flame which in its turn has caused an hallucination in the overwrought spirit of the poor mother.

The explanation is correct and exact, and science is quite right. But how much more consoling is it for that hapless mother, the hallucination which brought peace to the soul, than the cold explanation which would leave her in all the bitterness of sorrow!

Let us state another example. Above the heights of Amboto appears a heavy dark cloud presaging a storm. On its appearance the fishermen return precipitately to port; the field labourers, the traveller, and the shepherds all fly terrified back to their dwellings, and as they do so murmur, amid words of prayer, the strange words, *The lady of Amboto! the lady of Amboto!*

And who is this lady?

The wandering soul of a woman bereft of faith and conscience, who, after sacrificing to her ambition the love of a wife, that of a daughter, and even her hope of eternal salvation, commits the last and greatest crime--that of self-destruction--by casting herself down a precipice, and her spirit, in just expiation of so much sin, finds itself condemned to wail and wander for ever a victim to remorse among the peaks of Amboto. Her apparition is always followed by some great misfortune. The traces of her footprints are always marked with tears and blood, and, like to the birds of prey which are only aroused by the smell of blood, she foretells also the hour of calamity, and quits her haunts to revel in tears and wails.

On the other hand, a white lovely mist is seen to rise and hover over the top of Morumendi, and this mist becomes lost in space like a soft vapour. If on beholding this mist some become alarmed, this is soon succeeded by gleams of hope springing up in their hearts, and they hail the beneficent lady who comes to announce to them that, although the hours of trial are at hand, she will help them to surmount them. *Here comes the good lady! Here comes the good lady!* is heard from every lip blessing the spirit of the chaste and heroic maiden who sacrificing for her aged father her own happiness and affections and her very life, ended her lonely days in prayer on the rugged peaks of Morumendi.

The soul of the proud, unnatural daughter comes always accompanied by black clouds presaging disaster.

The apparition of the innocent maiden ever comes amid vapourous mists, white like her spotless soul, and announcing hope and peace.

The lady of Amboto symbolizes Ingratitude, ambition, and crime, and her spirit dwells in the midst of general execration, and is received with curses.

The lady of Morumendi symbolizes abnegation, virtue, innocence, and lives amid the blessings of the grateful hearts of all the people.

All this is fantastic and absurd, there is no doubt. But to the Basque it has been during twenty generations a moral lesson written with clouds upon the gigantic peaks of Amboto and Morumendi.

And similarly in all the other traditions which have been preserved, there is always discovered in their origin either a principle of morality, or the sacred cultus of the paternal hearth, or the passionate love of their mountains. That is to say, the three greatest and purest sentiments of humanity--the love of God, the love of home, and the love of the country--the three great virtues which the Romans admired in the Basques some twenty centuries ago These virtues have distinguished the race throughout that immense space of time, and these very virtues will still shine in the coming generations, although unfortunately without the vigorous energy of their forefathers.

And perchance--can it be doubted?--these popular legends have had no small share in preserving the character of the Basque race so distinctly, that at the present day they stand alone and unique amid the ruin and desolation which have befallen all other primitive races, retaining its language, customs, beliefs, and the same spirit which so eminently distinguished them in the midst of all those opulent ancient empires, the remembrance of which is fast becoming obliterated from the memory of the people.

Entone at the present day the song of Hanibal which our forefathers sang thirty centuries ago, or that of Lekovide in the time of Augustus Octavius, or that of Altabiscar during the epoch of Charlemagne, and the humblest shepherd of the mountains will understand it as though it had been composed for him. On the other hand, what people or race understands the Sagas of the SCALDOS, the poem of the Nibelung, the chants of Ossian, and the hymns of the Armenians? Only a few learned men who have made the languages which no longer exist objects of study. And this is not due solely to the fact that the language of those days is still preserved as that the spirit which distinguished the race has been perpetuated, and the people at the present day judge and feel and live in the same manner as they did in the ancient days of their glory.

By what other means but by tradition do we know the names of the heroic chieftains of that race of warriors which carried terror and dismay into the very centre of proud Rome--the Lekovides, Uchines, and Lartaunes?

What history has preserved the glorious names of Hernio, Gurutzeta, Orovioc, Betzaide, and others too numerous to mention?

By what explanation could we be able to comprehend better than by the *Canto of Alos* the imposing solemnity and the deep sentiment of the funeral ceremony of Gau-illa?

Truly, then, can it be said, that the nation which more completely gathers together the largest collection of traditions, ballads, and popular legends, must be the one possessing the most complete history.

For this reason throughout the German States has the prosecution of this branch of study been followed with interest and assiduity, and in France also with national spirit.

Hence, if this study is held to be one of such great importance by the two great nations which are at the head of the literary movements of the world, and that, moreover, possesses beautiful and multiplied histories written by the finest intellects with all the philosophical conditions which modern criticism exact--what interest must not a nation such as the Basque inspire, which has no chronicles or archives, inscriptions or any other of the indispensable elements required for forming such a vast work as this?

There remains, therefore, to us but one path open--the memory of the people.

Let us hasten to collect, each on his part, the materials necessary for this important object, and the day may dawn when some privileged genius shall bring to a conclusion the imperfect work which I have commenced of bringing forward before an enlightened English public the vast array of not only Basque legends, but the legends of many other provinces of Spain.

And let us hasten with all speed, for the gods are departing. Through an irreparable misfortune, which is not sufficiently deplored, this hapless nation or race is suffering in its depths a deep and laboured transformation. The levelling breath of the age is wresting from the heart of the Basques on a par with the superstitions in which they lived, their lofty sentiments and partriarchal customs; and the people, on apprehending by the light of new ideas the simple paucity of their beliefs experience a sad humiliation on perceiving their credulity and ignorance. In our day it is sad to say, even the most rustic husbandman appears ashamed to recount those tales which at one time he listened to with enthusiasm and with implicit faith; and on asking for any narrative he will look askance, suspecting that the interrogator may sneer at his simplicity.

Let it not be thought, however, that because we are enthusiastic for all ancient lore we cease to acknowledge the immense benefits humanity owes to illustration and the progress of modern times; but in this especial point, uniting ourselves for a moment to the ideas of the Basque people, let me ask, with what ideas and sentiments could the space be filled up in their history were we to tear down and scorn the beliefs and traditions, ideas and customs of that race which so largely contributed to their well-being for more than twenty centuries, imprinting on the character of the Basque that seal of wonderful originality which has always distinguished the race? That is to say, the admirable harmony which unites in them the most peaceful instincts with an heroic valour in dangers; of spontaneous submission to authority with an indomitable spirit of liberty; and lastly, a modest simplicity with an energetic aspiration for all that is grand.

But apart from all this the sad truth must be told the Basque of the present day, especially the generation that is rising up, does not feel the love and yearning for home and hearth felt by their elders, and those traditions and tales of their forefathers no longer satisfy his spirit. It is urgent, therefore, to gather together these legends from the generation which is fast passing away, else if we wait much longer we know not whether even a trace of their footprints will be in existence. Many traditions have already disappeared, losing along with them part of the precious treasures of our beloved country's history; but as this cannot now be remedied, let us repair the loss by collecting what remains, and preserve them with religious veneration, since they are the relics of the greatness, the virtues, and faith of our forefathers.

It is a recognized fact that the people inhabiting mountainous countries are all, more or less, given to believe in the marvellous or the supernatural, because nature presents herself in those lands under forms of greater beauty and grandeur, and thus offers to the imagination of the simple dwellers a more free scope for the marvellous. Such are the rugged shores of the Rhine strewn with the weird ruins of feudal castles; the mountains and lakes of Scotland; the broken rocks of the Hebrides, as well as the vast wild tracts of land of Emerald Erin, covered with an evergreen underwood. In some may be found *gnomes* or *ghosts*; in others, *white ladies* riding fantastic steeds; or *Peri*, or again *Will-o'-the-wisps*--but in all are found innumerable multitudes of mysterious beings whose cries or dances, games and aërial cavalcades, have been seen beneath the pale light of the moon, or among the mists, or the froth of waterfall, or torrent, or mountain stream, which, as it dashes and splashes up, form supposed canopies for the spirits inhabiting the waters, or hovering under the branches of the huge ancient trees of the forest.

Should any enlightened traveller sit down at the hospitable hearth of one of the dwellers of these countries and listen to the marvellous adventures narrated in perfect faith by the patriarch of the family, and listened to with the greatest respect and in deep silence by all his family and retainers; and should the said traveller interrupt the narrative by any movement or sign of incredulity, he would see the whole family rise up together and protest against such an act, not because of its discourtesy, but because it casts an injurious doubt, and such a doubt would lessen the importance of that district or village, should they not be able to boast of the existence of some of these mysterious beings, undefined it is true, but supposed ever to exert some direct influence on all the important events of their simple, monotonous life. And, to convince the traveller of the truth of what is advanced, some stalwart shepherd will assert that he has been awakened on a certain night by the light kiss of a white *Will-o'-the-wisp* which has dragged him out of his straw bed and carried him to a neighbouring wood, sore and tossed by the rapid whirls of some wild dance. The old man will add that he remembers how in his youth he saw the *While Lady* of the neighbouring castle pass on horseback across the wood, with a falcon fastened to her wrist, and accompanied by a retinue of hunters with bugle-horns, and leading hunting dogs.

After these asseverations, follow the tales of the aged mistress of the house, who will relate how she saw *with her own eyes* a wilful imp spilling the salt, turning over the pots and kettles, and even carrying its audacity to the point of fastening an old rag to the tail of the most venerable cat of the house.

In view of, to them, such unimpeachable proofs the visitor is bound to agree with them, that in truth *ghosts* and *peri*, *white ladies* and *Will-o'-the-wisps* do exist, and in this manner he will once more win the good opinion of his hosts.

I am of opinion that it is better to allow these good people to live in peace with their superstitions, which do no harm to any one, leaving to time the work of undeceiving them, than to put ourselves forward as reformers among them by endeavouring to root up their simple beliefs. Moreover, the people that from their simplicity believe in all these things are found as a rule to be more virtuous, peaceful, and honest, better disposed to observe religious duties and precepts, and more obedient to the laws of their respective governments, because these simple beliefs prepare them in a certain manner to accept other beliefs which are of greater importance and interest.

And I go further than this: how would they pass the long evenings of winter were they deprived of the marvellous stories which they narrate in peace and good fellowship, sitting around the fire, and that serve them as food for their imagination and of repose and relaxation after their hard day's rough work in the fields?

Let us bear in mind that, at least during the time they narrate these marvellous fables and stories, they are happy and contented. Therefore let us not embitter with our scepticism the pleasure these people enjoy.

The tract or range of land and mountains which comprises the Basque Provinces contains mountains similar to those of Scotland, hills as green as may be found in Ireland, rivers with shores as rugged as are those of Germany, with bleak coasts as huge and inhospitable as are the coasts of the Hebrides. This country, topographically so similar to the above-mentioned nations, possesses a people dowered with an imagination as vivid as theirs, inclined to create fantastic beings known under the name of *Lamiæ*, inhabiting their tempestuous coasts; *Bassa-jaon*, or *jauna*, dwelling in their interminable woods; *Mailagarrys* amid the luxuriant forests; and *Sorguiñas* on the solitary plains and in the fissures opened by the force of the mountain torrents,

The legends and historical traditions of a people *sui generis*, possessing a language at once magnificent, original, and similar to none, a brilliant poetic imagination, fired with a love which amounts almost to idolatry for their mountains, a deeply-rooted religious faith, simple patriarchal habits, extraordinary progress, undoubted virtues, and an admirable administration worthy of being imitated, must, I feel assured, prove of interest to the English public, which is ever ready to recognize and acknowledge the grandeur and virtues of foreign nations, and take an interest even in their fairy and popular stories.

M. M.

Aquelarre

I.

IN the territory which stands between the towns of Zuggaramurdi and Echalar, a mountainous tract covered with woods, crossed by rivulets, and divided by narrow and very deep valleys, will be found, isolated and darksome, the mountain of Aquelarre, overgrown with brambles and thorns, and surrounded by rocks and waterfalls.

The position of the mountain and its conical form invites the attention of geologists visiting these rugged places; and in effect it is curious to notice that while other mountains, branches of the Pyrenees, are joined to-ether by defiles which form undulations full of various accidents, in some, of soft, ev-er-green brows, while in other instances their heights are perfect plains, and in some again peaked Aquelarre is roughly different from. the general form of these mountains, so that it stands an exception in the midst of them.

It is said that "Ariel," the titular genius of the Biscayans, one day stretched out his powerful arm and wrenched from its base this singular mountain, placing it at a distance from its companion, so that they should not become contaminated by any contact with this accursed mountain. In fact Aquelarre is an accursed mountain. If you believe it not, remark the colour of the brambles which cover its enormous sides. It is not a green that pleases the sight, the colour in which the noble oak clothes its branches. Neither is it the silvery hue of the white poplar. Much less is it the brilliant green of the handsome beech-tree. Nor does it approach to the green which covers the cherry, the pear, and the nut-trees, full of white, fragrant flowers, in whose salyx shines the drop of dew, like a pure diamond.

The colour of the brushwood of Aquelarre, sombre, lugubrious, darksome, resembles the gigantic peak of Lithuania, or of the cypress which grows in the fissures of the stony hills of Arabia Petrea--a funereal sinister hue which saddens the spirit and represses the expansion of soul of the poet, that in a rapture contemplates the sumptuous gifts and graces of nature in the woods, or the smiling and simple glory of the flower-strewn valleys.

Why this notable contrast? Why this dark phantom in the midst of such beautifully bedecked nature? Because all things that are in contact with the genius of evil carry with them the seal of reprobation, substituting for their ancient beauty forms at once repugnant and loathsome.

Aquelarre finds itself in this sad state. Its heights are frequented by the prince of darkness, and in the crevices of the mountains are repeated the echoes of the irreligious songs which are entoned in his praise.

Many in terror and fear have heard these songs resounding in the mountains, and breaking the majestic silence of the night.

There are some who have seen columns of black smoke rising, and have perceived a nauseous smell emanating from the confines of this accursed mountain, and have with reason conjectured, that the smoke was produced by the holocausts offered to the genius of evil by his wicked worshippers in some mysterious sacrifices.

Nevertheless, who were these spirits? From whence do they come to celebrate their nocturnal revels?

The simple dweller of the mountains shrugs his shoulders on being asked these questions, and contents himself with replying laconically--"*Eztaquit*" ("I do not know").

Suddenly a report was spread from mouth to mouth, and which gained ground and soon became general, to the effect, that the discovery had been made of what passed on the heights of the accursed mountain by a child.

Behold how tradition tells us this was effected.

Izar and Lañoa were two orphan children; the first was seven years of age and the latter nine. These poor children, true wandering bards, frequented the mountains, earning a livelihood by singing ballads and national airs in sweet infantile voices, in return for a bed of straw and a cupful of meal. Throughout the district these children were known and loved on account of their sad state, as well as for their graceful forms and winning ways.

There was, however, a difference between the two. Izar, the younger brother, was fair as jasper; his long hair fell in curls, pale as the stems of the maize, down his shoulders and back; his eyes were of the purest sky-blue, while from them shot glances at once sweet and suppliant of irresistible force; his lips were red as the flower of the wild pomegranate, around which hovered a smile as gentle as the light puff of an expiring breeze, and, on contracting them, two dimples appeared in his rosy cheeks. Izar was the more patient of the brothers, the meeker, and the more beautiful; his voice had a purer tone, and for that reason was the favourite of the inhabitants of the mountains.

Lañoa was as handsome as his brother, but Nature had dowered him with a different style of beauty. His figure was more lithe, and his limbs of stronger make; the looks he cast out of his black eyes were haughty--at times even arrogant and full of daring. The way he curled his upper lip revealed a passionate, proud character, his hair was black with the bluish shade seen on the feathers of the raven; his long eye-lashes somewhat softened the fire of his eagle eye. Nevertheless, Lañoa was a good lad, and loved his younger brother, notwithstanding that at times he would treat him roughly.

It was on a sad, cloudy day in November that these two were walking towards Aranaz, crossing with difficulty the mountains enveloped in a fog, and covered with snow.

Izar grew very tired climbing the heights, and the poor child had not the courage to ask his brother to help him up. Lañoa, on his part, was not disposed to offer any help, however much in his heart he desired Izar to ask assistance, which he could then give without to his pride.

13

"Poor fellow, he is tired," he would say to himself; "but he does not wish to humble himself to ask me to help him up. If he expects me to offer it----."

Musing in this way, he increased his speed, thus lengthening the distance which separated him from Izar. The latter endeavoured to reach him by taking great strides to do so; but he could barely keep on his delicate feet, until by a great effort he sought to keep within hearing of his voice.

All at once a gust of wind brought down large masses of wet, heavy snow into the defile through which walked the brothers, and Lañoa was compelled to suspend the rapid speed he had sustained, and thus enabled Izar in a short time to come up to him.

"What shall we do?" he timidly asked.

"Do what you please, lazy boy," Lañoa replied, roughly; "for my part I shall continue my walk as soon as the fog clears away a little."

"Very well, my brother," replied Izar, gently but meanwhile sit down at my feet and I will cover you with my capusay, [2] for you are in such a heat with your efforts."

"Women and lazy children like yourself require to be sheltered from the wind; as for me, I am a man, and I am not frightened with the cold."

Saying this, he uncovered his head, and exposed his wavy hair to the freezing gusts of the north wind.

"What are you doing, my brother?" cried Izar, rising from the broken rock upon which he had sat, and covering with his cap the head of Lañoa. "Oh, please let me cover you from the cold," he continued. "I well know that you are stronger than I am, and for that very reason should you take care of yourself, so that you may help me that am so weak."

"Be off!" cried Lañoa, pushing his brother away, who slipped and fell to the ground. And with bare head he resolutely commenced anew his march across the deep, cold snow.

Izar did not reply a word, nor did he even utter a cry of pain as his head was wounded by falling upon a stone. He rose up to renew his good work of abnegation and charity; and then he noticed with deep sorrow that his brother had disappeared from view. He ran in all directions, calling him with loud cries; but the fog, was so dense that he was unable to find him. Then, half dead with fatigue, in despair, and shivering with the cold, the poor child looked around him, and perceived through the fog that at a short distance from him stood an immense tree, and that its trunk was hollow.

Night was rapidly closing in, covering with its dark mantle these solitary places. The fog grew more heavy and damp; and instead of dispersing, remained stationary, clinging to the branches of the trees, and descending like the waters of a stream into the marshes and valleys.

From the hollow of the tree in which our young hero had taken shelter could be seen an extensive tract of land covered with a white mist; in places it remained still like the waters of a lake; in others it rose and fell like the sea waves that break on the rocky promontories.

In that veritable ocean of fog could be perceived here and there black points like so many dark islands, which no doubt were the peaked heights of that range of mountains.

The silence was deep and solemn. The night was fast increasing in darkness.

In the distance, and above the fog, could be seen a yellow line of light presaging the rising of the moon, which at that time of the year was of opaque brilliancy, and more so seen in that atmosphere full of fog and mist.

Izar understood, from what he could descry, that he was standing on the top of a mountain; so quitting his shelter he reconnoitred the surroundings.

The protecting tree stood in the centre of a small plain, surrounded on all sides by thick shrubs and brushwood, so tangled and close that he could discover no opening or path by which he could possibly descend from its height down to the base.

How did that lost child find his way into such a spot?

He could not tell.

Feeling hungry and thirsty, and, moreover, finding himself in a spot which was totally unknown to him, he began to cry from anguish and fear; but at length, convinced that all this was unavailing, he returned to the worm-eaten hollow of that tree, fully determined to pass the night in its hospitable shelter. He fervently commended his soul to God; he thought in sadness of his. mother, who had loved him so tenderly, and he prayed to the All-powerful to deliver his elder brother of whatever danger he might find himself in. Having done this, he sat down, and wrapping himself as comfortably as he could in his poor coat, he huddled up in his hiding-place, and the sleep of innocence very soon closed his eyelids.

At the moment when he placed his soul and body trustingly in the safe keeping of a God full of goodness, the heavens were rent open and an angel beautiful as are all the angels, descended in a rapid flight and alighted on the branches of the tree. Then he extended his white wings, and with loving solicitude watched the sleep of the innocent child.

For a length of time did Izar sleep calmly and sweetly under the loving care of the angel. At length he was suddenly aroused by a singular and incessant uproar which seemed to fill space. He cautiously peeped out of the hollow trunk of the tree, and an incomprehensible spectacle presented itself to his view. The moon was shining on the plain, and, casting a pale reflection over space, imparted a weird appearance and fantastic form to all objects.

From the point in the heavens occupied by the planet of night, and extending along the vast line of the horizon, the tints were becoming more and more sombre, passing from light grey to the deepest black. Out of the four cardinal points of the horizon rose up four extremely long lines of fantastic shadows, from which issued terrible unearthly cries, and these shadows with astounding rapidity all travelled to meet in a concentric point. This point was actually the very plain which we have just described. To depict in words the strange cavalcade upon which these fantastic shadows were mounted, would

15

be a work superior to human ability. The one would press between its flesh-less knees the skeleton of a mammoth of huge proportions; the other rode a horrible monstrous owl; others, again, divided the air riding on broomsticks; while some were perched on the backs of serpents bearing enormous wings, long tails, and with brilliant eyes.

All these shadows joined one another until the four lines formed an immeasurable chain. And thus they whirled until they gathered together at a distance of about a hundred feet from the ground; then they greeted one another with frenzied cries, ringing shrieks of laughter, deafening shouts, and hideous yells. After this they began a circular flight in a confused disorder, and little by little they began to descend to the ground.

The astonishment and terror of Izar increased when he perceived that all these shadows were so many forms of decrepit old women. Their faces, blackened and wrinkled, were repulsive, while their hideous bodies inspired disgust, their short matted hair and fleshless limbs were truly fearful to see. The terror which all this scene inspired in the heart of Izar who was an unwilling witness, increased to a terrible degree when he noticed that all these women were preparing to execute some unearthly dance, taking one another's hands, and forming a large circle around the hollow tree in which he had taken refuge. And, what was more strange still to him, was the fact that this immense crowd fitted perfectly in the plain without requiring to widen its circuit or to diminish the size of their figures. As Izar had feared, it was not long before the dance commenced. At first this dance was of slow movements, and all kept time stepping together, now on one foot now on the other.

Little by little the leaps became more violent, the turns more rapid, until at length this nameless dance turned into a sort of whirlwind, increasing in speed, until it caused dizziness to attempt to follow the movements.

Jumps, cries, terrible contortions, turns--all were supernatural, all horrible to the sight, all was a confused, incomprehensible jargon to the ear.

Poor Izar could no longer support that spectacle, and he fell fainting to the ground. When he recovered consciousness the moon had disappeared. The night was pitch dark, a sepulchral silence reigned throughout the plain. He looked out again from his hiding-place, judging that these fiendish women who had so alarmed him must have disappeared; but he perceived in terror that they still occupied the same spot as before, but in more strange attitudes, if possible. They were all ranged in a circle, huddled up close together, around a throne of ebony, upon which was seen calmly sitting an enormous he-goat, From this throne gleamed a few rays of yellow light, the only light which illumined the scene. The old women were successively approaching the throne, and as they did so they each respectfully kissed the hairy cloven foot of the goat. Then, after this long ceremony was concluded, the goat shook his head, and one by one each of these creatures commenced to relate what she had done.

16

Izar, horrified at being compelled to listen to their hideous narratives of premeditated deaths, mutilation of babes, profanation of cemeteries, and other crimes, was once more about to faint away with horror, when he heard a sweet voice which seemed to come from among the branches of the tree, and which pronounced his name. Astonished at this, he arose, and raising his eyes to the direction from whence came the voice, he saw among the branches a young man of celestial beauty, who was gazing upon Izar with tender, loving looks.

"Listen, and do not fear," the young man said, "for I am here to guard and watch over you."

Then Izar bent his ear to listen to what was said by the women, and he heard the following conversation.

"All my sisters," one of the witches was saying in a hissing voice, "have obeyed your commands. There was not a single one of them who did not send you, oh sovereign master, some victims, but I challenge any of them to do what I can."

"Speak, my daughter," murmured the goat: "I well know that you are one of my most devoted worshippers."

"You know, my lord," continued the witch, "that the grand reigning Duke of F------ and his lady are both zealous Christians, faithful and true, and you are also aware that they have a daughter lovely as the sun, whom they idolize. What a joy to me to make this beautiful creature die by inches; to wither that flower in all its youth and freshness, and to sow despair in the hearts of her parents, and so deliver them up to your powerful temptations! Would it not be a masterly stroke to kill them also after two or three months of cruel sufferings? What would it cost you, my lord, to impel them to destroy their own life?"

A horrible grimace, which no doubt was intended to be a smile of satisfaction, overspread the countenance of the goat, and his eyes darted gleams of fire impossible to describe.

"Should you do so," replied the author of evil, "you will become the best beloved of my daughters."

"Well, then, give me my reward, my lord. It is now a week since the princess began to suffer, and no one is able to discover the cause of her complaint, and still less can they find the remedies to effect her cure."

"Are you not afraid that some one will discover it?

"No, my lord, because the spell which binds her consists in the existence of an enormous toad which lies concealed under a broken statue, which has been abandoned and cast away in a corner of the garden of the ducal residence. So long as this toad is not destroyed, the sickness will follow its course and the princess will die."

"This that you tell me pleases me greatly, Bazzioti, and I desire to have frequent and exact accounts given me of what happens. I give you my thanks for what you do," continued the genius of evil, "and I summon you to come next Saturday."

Saying this, the evil one shook his head; a terrible thunder-clap was heard, and the throne disappeared along with he who sat upon it. All things became enveloped in a complete obscurity.

Soon after this Izar heard the noise of the witches rising up and taking to flight on the winds, and by the now dim light of the moon he descried the fantastic line of shadows that in silence were departing towards the points of the horizon from whence they came, and slowly disappeared among the mass of black clouds.

Izar then looked up to the branches of the tree and saw there the young man who had bidden him have no fear. This angelic youth then said to him, "Fulfil your mission as I have fulfilled mine!" Then, spreading his wings, he rose to the sky, casting behind him sparks of brilliant light, and leaving a celestial fragrance which comforted the child's benumbed limbs and instilled warmth and courage into his heart.

II.

A month had passed since Izar had been a witness to this strange conventicle. Full of faith in the words of the angel, he walked on to perform the charitable act which was so much in harmony with his good heart. Determined to overcome all the obstacles which might beset his path, he continued his march night and day towards Italy, for it was in one of its small States that the Grand Duke of F------ reigned.

How was he able to traverse great nations without means, and without even knowing the languages which were spoken in them? Tradition does not tell us anything concerning this particular. What is affirmed by the inhabitants of the Basque Provinces is, that he reached his destination and to the gates of the palace of the reigning grand duke.

It would certainly have been a difficult feat for our young adventurer to succeed in approaching the person of so high a personage, had not the duchess, who was returning from a neighbouring church, whither she had resorted to pray for the restoration of the health of her daughter, at that moment entered into the palace, and, noticing that a poor child was at the gates, supposed it was to solicit alms that he had come; so she beckoned to him and gave him a silver coin, saying, "Take this alms, poor child, and ask our dear Lord to grant that my daughter may be restored to health. The prayers of an innocent child are very pleasing to God, and will assuredly obtain the boon from Him which he refuses to us."

"Is it your daughter that is sick?" sweetly asked Izar.

"Yes, my own darling daughter."

"Very well, then," Izar rejoined, "I will cure her."

"You?" cried the duchess, in astonishment. "Poor child! perhaps you do not know that the first physicians of the land and the cleverest have despaired of effecting a cure?"

"I certainly was not aware of this; but all I know is that I have come here expressly to cure the princess, and cure her I will!"

The duchess, mute with astonishment, looked fixedly at Izar, who stood there surrounded by her servitors, yet calm, erect, but with a modest bearing, and uncovered head, his golden hair falling over his; shoulders in curls.

The clear look in his eyes manifested truth and candour; the smile that hovered around his lips was so gentle and winning, that the noble lady, after consulting for a few moments with the ladies of honour who accompanied her, and who all tacitly assented to the duchess allowing the child to carry out the purport of his words, took Izar by the hand and led him up the sumptuous stairs of the palace.

While this singular scene was taking place at the palace gates the duke sat by the bedside of his dying child.

The invalid was about eight years of age. Her large, almond-shaped eyes had already lost the light and life which was the delight of her parents, and were sinking in their sockets. A dark circle could be seen around her eyelids, and the extreme pallor of her delicate face clearly indicated the approaching end of that sweet flower prematurely fading away. The parched lips had lost their rosy colour. It was distressing to gaze upon that painful scene.

Nothing could be more terrible than the sorrow of the father as he witnessed the slow agony of his beloved daughter. A sorrow mute, it is true, but deep; a grief which, finding no vent in tears, was all the more fearful in its results. Because a father, besides endeavouring to stifle the grief which anguishes him, has at the same time to alleviate another pain--the sorrow of the mother.

At this moment the door of the sick chamber is opened, and the duchess was just entering, leading Izar by the hand, and followed by her ladies and pages, who, attracted by the novelty of the affair, had come to see the end of all this singular episode.

Izar did not manifest the least astonishment while treading the soft carpets of that regal house, or when crossing the chambers covered with damasks and velvets, gold and marbles.

On seeing him thus calmly following the duchess, without manifesting the least surprise or curiosity, and without opening his rosy lips, except to smile whenever she looked at him, none would have suspected for a moment that this lovely golden-haired boy had passed days and nights walking through woods covered with briars, or that he had slept under no better shelter or bed than the blackened thatch of rough cabins and huts of the Basque mountains and upon the hard ground. But this circumstance did not escape the observation of the duchess, and this very fact lit up a ray of hope in her heart.

Scarcely had the duchess entered the chamber than she was met by the duke, who, going to meet her, said in a sad tone: "My lady, we must lose all hope now; our beloved daughter will assuredly die!"

"Oh, my friend, be comforted," she replied; "who knows but she will yet be spared?"

"Alas! no, I have no hope whatever," said the duke "she is dying, my lady, she is fast dying."

The duchess then turned towards Izar, who stood behind her, and as she did so noticed that he was casting a look full of smiles towards the duke.

"Whoever you are," the duchess exclaimed, as she took Izar by the hand and drew him close to her, "is it true that you will cure our daughter?"

"I have come to do so," quietly replied Izar.

"You perceive," said the duchess to her husband, "that there is still some hope left."

"Who is this boy?" asked the duke, greatly astonished.

"I do not know," replied the duchess; "I met him on my return from the church, and on asking him to pray to God for our child, he replied that he had come to cure her!"

"Can this be so?" exclaimed the duke.

"It is," replied Izar.

"Who are you?" rejoined the duke. "Perchance are you an angel sent by God to comfort us?

"I am a poor orphan, my lord." Where do you come from? "I have come from distant lands."

To cure my daughter?" demanded the sorrow-stricken father.

"Yes, that has been the only object of my journey, and I have walked the whole way, and day and night for a month."

All the persons present at this singular interview gave a cry of surprise. The duke passed his hand across his brow like a man who is mentally agitated; then, after a few moments of thought, he took his resolve, and led the way towards where the sick child lay unconscious and fast dying away, and made a sign for Izar to approach.

The extraordinary replies of the boy, coupled with his self-possession, greatly excited the curiosity of all who, witnessed the scene, and the ladies and servitors were gathered together in a group at the door of the bedchamber.

Izar approached the bed, and in silence gazed for some time upon the unconscious form of the princess, who scarcely gave signs of life.

"Here is the invalid--can you cure her?" said the duke to Izar.

Izar did not reply. He stood contemplating her. At length he murmured, in a scarcely audible voice--

"So this is the flower that is to wither away!"

The general anxiety was great.

Suddenly all the bystanders uttered a cry of joy. The princess was smiling sadly: certainly that smile was the first sign of life she had shown for days. The duchess, in obedience to a sudden impulse, fell on her knees before the boy, and, with a look on her face which it is impossible to describe, cried, in a tone of voice that made them all tremble--

"In the name of God, save our Sophia!"

"Rise up, poor sorrowing mother," replied Izar, in a solemn voice; "I have come to save your daughter, and save her I will!"

"Do you hear, my daughter?" said the duchess, pressing to her lips the icy hand of the dying child. "This lad has come to cure you."

The sick girl opened her eyes, from which the light had almost departed, smiled faintly, and put out her hand to the orphan boy.

The excitement of those present reached its climax. The duke then placed both his hands on the curly head of that orphan boy, and in a solemn voice said, "I swear by my ducal crown that if you save my daughter you shall be her brother!"

Izar thanked him by an inclination of the head and swiftly left the chamber, requesting that none should follow him. All present respectfully made way for him to pass.

The boy descended the stairs and went into the garden. He searched every nook and corner, and the most retired spots under trees, until, after a diligent search, he discovered, hidden away, a broken statue, covered with overgrown masses of tangled thorns and briars. He cleared away, as well as he could, all these weeds, and by a great effort was able to raise the broken statue, when, to his great delight, he found the loathsome toad, which, on being discovered, glared at Izar with fierce, wild looks.

Izar jumped on the toad and crushed it dead. Then he quickly returned to the sick-room, where all were awaiting the return of the lad, anxious at his long absence.

When they heard the door opened, and saw that Izar had returned, every face beamed with joy. They awaited the mysterious child, and there he stood before them, calm and as self-possessed as ever. He approached the bed. of the sick girl, and said--

"Sophia, my sister, do you hear me?"

"Yes," replied the princess; "I no longer feel that heavy weight here--here, on my chest."

"Oh, my God! may you be praised cried the duchess, shedding a torrent of tears my Sophia is saved!"

"Do you hear what your mother says, my sister? Rise up, for now you are cured."

The princess rose up slowly and sat on her bed, then looked around her as one awaking from a heavy sleep, rubbed her eyes, and said, smiling, "Yes, I am well."

Then the duke clasped Izar in his arms and said--

"In the name of the all-powerful God of heaven, I adopt as my own son this orphan, who has shed so much happiness on our house. Do you consent to this, duchess?"

The only reply of the grateful lady was to kneel before the orphan lad, and to say--

"My son, bless your mother."

* * * * * *

The fame of this marvellous event soon spread throughout Italy, traversed the Alps, and became the theme for the *improvisatores* of the provinces, who narrated it in tender strophes. From thence it passed on to the Basque bards, and these again so distributed the legend and tale in the neighbourhood of the mountains, that the dwellers and inhabitants of the surrounding districts of Aquelarre, where this story had its first beginning, within a few months were well acquainted with all its details.

III.

We said in the first part of this narrative that Lañoa, after pushing back his young brother, started off in spite of the dense fog. He very soon became aware that Izar was not following him, and he stopped in his walk, hoping that in a short time he should be able to rejoin him. But after some considerable time had passed, and there were no signs of his brother returning, he began to feel uneasy, and commenced to call him, in hopes that he should hear his voice. He called his name many times, but all was in vain--there was no response. The silence of the mountains remained unbroken by any reply, and seeing that it was useless to call him, as the fog prevented his voice from piercing space, he felt very anxious, and returned to the spot where he had left him. But the child was no longer there, and then a violent fit of despair and remorse took possession of Lañoa.

He wept bitterly for his brother whom he had forsaken: the excited imagination of the youth conjured him dying of cold and hunger on those bleak mountains, imploring his help and accusing him of unfeeling, harsh conduct.

Poor Lañoa became desperate: he ran all about the place, calling Izar in frenzied cries; then he threw himself on the ground, tearing his hair. Yet all was in vain. He spent the long night on that rock, a prey to fever and remorse.

On the following day he searched throughout the neighbouring mountains, but he could discover no vestige or track of footsteps to indicate to him that a human being had passed that way. Then a deep melancholy settled on his spirit, and from that day no one ever heard him sing his favourite ballads. He became a. misanthrope and a savage; he fled from every one, and hapless he who would have the hardihood to ask him tidings of Izar!

Five months passed away in this wandering, solitary manner, ever searching the woods and lonely places; and the shepherds who knew him began to suspect that he had committed the crime of Cain.

When these suspicions began to gain ground, the ballad and tale about the life of Izar, and the beautiful mysterious Sophia, were already sung in good Basque verses. This ballad was an exact narrative of all that had occurred from the separation of the brothers to the adoption of the orphan boy by the grand reigning duke.

It was not long before this song reached the ears of Lañoa, to whom it afforded an immense joy, and relieved his heart of its heavy weight of sorrow.

He would follow those who sang this ballad, and, when it was ended, used to ask humbly that it be repeated.

His character suddenly altered: he became gentle and tractable. Meantime the beauty of spring had succeeded the bleakness of winter, the sweet perfumed breeze of April to the violent snowstorms of December. The mountains were clothed in freshness and verdure, and the birds were saluting with joyful songs the return of their season of love. "Aquelarre" alone remained sad and bleak as ever in the midst of that joyous nature. It was said that Aquelarre, jealous of the universal joy of nature, took delight in saddening the smiling scene by showing a sinister face, dark, and bleak in opposition, and as a striking contrast to the merry, laughing aspect of its neighbouring mountain companions. No bird sang on its trees; no playful roe ever climbed the rugged sides of the accursed mountain. All was solitude; all things were silent.

One day, at the twilight hour of evening, the shepherds of the valleys perceived in fear and astonishment that on the solitary heights of Aquelarre wandered a human form. Struck by the oblique rays of the setting sun, this form acquired gigantic proportions. Side by side with this figure was seen another of similar form and size, which faithfully followed all its movements. This was simply, the effect of an optical illusion, a phenomenon sufficiently common to those elevated regions where objects acquire colossal dimensions that become duplicated by the refraction of the solar rays crossing subtle masses of vapours.

Nevertheless, the simple shepherds ignore all this, and only see in that phenomena a warning for them to be on their guard against some coming evil. Moreover, fearful lest the night should surprise them in the immediate neighbourhood of the accursed mountain, in which, so they said, some sinister event of ill omen was being prepared, they hastened to collect together all their cattle, and shut themselves up in their huts and cabins.

The solitary figure that wandered on the top of Aquelarre was Lañoa. From the moment that he heard the ballad which narrated the history of his brother, he was assailed by a yearning wish to see Izar, but his pride resisted this desire, and deceived him in respect to the passion which domineered over him, by saying, "No, no; I cruelly abandoned him when he was poor and weak. I should not, now that he is rich and in position, go and seek him. When, like Izar, I shall have performed some generous noble act, then will I go to him, ask his pardon, and I know that he will pardon me, he is so good. I shall go up to the accursed mountain and listen for some secret spoken in the conventicle and then I will set to work."

It were necessary for any one who fostered such a thought as this, and moreover decided to carry it out, be dowered. with supernatural courage, and a strength of character above all proof; and Lañoa the bold most certainly possessed these qualities in a high degree. Another motive existed besides the above to impel him to attempt such an undertaking. It was vanity.

"What!" he used to say to himself, "shall I be less than my brother? He so weak--I so strong? He so gentle and meek--I so brave and hardy? No, no; I will ascend the rugged mountain, and challenge all the dangers which may beset me, until I attain to my end at any cost!"

The night was approaching, and Lañoa, following the route described in the ballad, found the tree, and concealed himself in its hollow trunk. It chanced that it was Saturday, and therefore the night set aside for assembling a conventicle. And so it happened. Towards midnight Lañoa began to hear a strange incessant noise that each moment approached nearer. He began to tremble when he descried the long lines of fantastic shadows which were directing their course towards the spot where he lay concealed. A cold perspiration ran down his forehead when the shadows saluted each other and formed the confused whirling dance that had so greatly surprised Izar. The cries and fiendish laughter of the witches increased his terror, and when at length he saw them descend on to the plain, and was able to distinguish their repugnant forms, the poor lad knew not what to do. The witches commenced their unearthly dances, and Lañoa was bitterly repenting that he had lent a willing ear to the counsels of pride. However, the evil was done, and now there was no help for it but to bear the consequences of his dire mistake, and he resolved to await as calmly as he could the unravelling of this fearful drama.

He had not long to wait. A fearful detonation shook the mountain to its base, and was quickly followed by the appearance of an ebony throne, and seated upon this throne was a figure, the most horrible that human eyes had ever beheld. The head of the prince of darkness was of an enormous size; his eyes, which were glaring and wide open, resembled the burning crater of a volcano; immense ears fell down on his shoulders; while out of the mouth, bereft of lips, issued volumes of dense smoke, across which could be descried now and again rows of long yellow pointed teeth. His hands and feet were covered with sharp nails, curved and long. The rest of his body corresponded to the hideousness of his countenance.

He cast a ferocious glance at the numerous retinue which tremblingly awaited the commands of their sovereign, and in a deep, cavernous voice cried out: "Bazzoti! Bazzoti!"

One of the witches that were huddled together then rose and placed herself opposite the throne of ebony.

"Ha! ha!" exclaimed the genius of evil. "What became of all your fine promises, you deceitful one?"

"They could not be carried out," tremblingly replied the witch.

"Listen," rejoined the one who sat on the throne: "the princess was cured, and her parents, far from thinking of destroying themselves through despair, each day are happier, and idolize more and more their child and my direst enemy!"

"Lord!" murmured the witch, half dead with fear.

"Silence!" replied the devil. "As I see that you are of no use to me in this world, go, and await me in the next."

Saying this, he struck the ground with his foot, and the witch disappeared down a deep pit which opened at his feet.

The other witches lowered their heads to the very ground, and remained silent.

"Now," he added, "I shall proceed to examine the tree."

Lañoa trembled from head to foot on hearing those words, and judged that he was lost. And indeed very quickly did he feel that he was being grasped by a number of these witches, who commenced to torture him in every way, and with Satanic mirth carried him bodily to the foot of the throne of the prince of darkness,

"Ha! so here we have another inquisitive mortal, it appears!" he cried, making a horrible grimace. "Approach, you profane one, approach!"

Lañoa in that terrible situation made a supreme effort, and assumed an expression on his countenance of satirical jesting,

"It appears that you do not fear us?" continued Lusbel, grinding his teeth.

Lañoa as his only reply contemptuously shrugged his shoulders.

It was a terrible wrestling that which was imminent between the lad, who had as his only weapon of defence his character of iron, and Lusbel armed with all the powers of hell.

"What were you doing in that tree?" he asked, after looking fixedly at Lañoa for a considerable time.

"I was deriding you," replied Lañoa, laughing.

"Profanation!" roared the witches.

"Silence! silence!" cried Satan; and the witches were hushed. "So you were deriding me?" he asked, after a moment of silence.

"Yes, I was, by my faith!"

"Do you perchance think that any one has ever been able to boast that he has derided me with impunity?" rejoined Lusbel.

"Yes, I do, seeing that my brother has done so with a good result," replied Lañoa.

"Oh! oh! so you are brother to the one who saved the life of the Italian princess?"

Lañoa did not reply.

"Answer quickly, cursed one!" said the witch nearest to him.

Lañoa turned quick as thought, grasped the witch by the hair of her head, threw her down on the ground, and placed his foot across her throat, then folded his arms in a defiant manner, and looked fixedly at Satan.

The latter remained perfectly stupefied on witnessing this rapid action, and to behold the imperturbable calm of the lad.

"By my kingship, lad, but you interest me," he at length said.

"Well, if I interest you, I on my part thoroughly despise you!" replied Lañoa.

"You dare to despise me?"

"Yes, I do!"

"You say this because you are not aware who I am!"

The lad curled his lip in sign of supreme contempt.

"Approach, if you dare, and touch my hand," he added, as he extended a hand armed with sharp nails.

Lañoa pushed aside with his foot the loathsome form of the witch, and fearlessly took the hand of Satan.

"Does it burn you?" he asked.

"I do not feel any heat," replied Lañoa, with the most perfect indifference; but nevertheless the lad's hair had stood on end when it felt the contact of that scorching hand.

"It is passing strange!" murmured Lusbel.

"You can well perceive," rejoined Lañoa, "that I do not fear you!"

"I own to that, certainly," he replied, releasing the hand of the youth, "but nevertheless that is no proof that you despise me."

"Do you wish for a proof?" arrogantly demanded L ah o a.

"Let us have one, certainly."

"There you have one!" cried the youth, and he spat at the face of Lusbel.

To describe the expression of fiendish rage which appeared on the monstrous countenance of Satan is not given to any pen to do. He uttered a roar, in comparison of which the violent eruption of a volcano would be no more than a soft melody. He wrathfully rose from his throne, grasped the boy in his clutches, and cast him headlong, like to a catapult, down the precipice which stands more than a league from that spot. The body of Lañoa rebounded and fell down the fearful descent a lifeless form, but his soul, purified in that trial rose up to heaven.

* * * * * *

Since then the above-mentioned precipice is known under the appellation of *Infernu erreca*, and the shepherds of the mountains affirm that at the hour of midnight on all Saturdays, with the exception of Easter Eve, there is heard rising up from that depth a tender wailing, and a noise resounds similar to that which is produced by the falling of a body.

[1] *Aquelarre*. A word composed of *larre*, pasture land, and *Aquerra*, buck goat; hence the word *Aquelarre* signifies the *pasture land of the goat*. It is well known that this animal figures in all the conventicles of witches as representing the Evil One.

[2] *Capusay*. A sort of dalmatic of very thick cloth furnished with a hood.

Arguiduna

I.

ALONG the winding stony road that leads from the valley of Urnieta to the gate of Arricarte, walked Juan de Azcue, followed by a retinue of robust huntsmen, with bows slung to their shoulders, and leashed mastiffs.

From the opposite side of the gate of Arricarte, and following a more devious rough path than the already mentioned road, came another similar retinue of huntsmen and dogs headed by Roman de Alzate. This veteran knight was bending his steps towards the same spot as Juan de Azcue, an aged yet hale man.

The two old men seemed to have become youthful again, so firmly did they step, and so rapid was their pace.

When both had reached to within a short distance of Arricarte they stopped and bade the huntsmen advance.

Those belonging to the retinue of Azcue were the first to arrive at the place of meeting.

"Are you of the house of Alzate?" they asked.

"Yes, we are. And are you of the retinue of Azcue?" the advancing troop demanded.

"Yes. Do you come in peace and good-will?"

"Yes, we do."

"In that case you are welcome."

They then unfurled small white flags, waved them in the air, and at that signal both chiefs advanced to the gateway.

"The peace of God be with you, Juan," said he of Alzate, uncovering his white head.

"I desire the same to you, Roman," replied he of Azcue, as he also removed his cap.

The retinues of the two chiefs saluted each other in silence.

"The words of the venerable *cura* opened my heart to reconciliation. I bless God that He has prolonged my life, that so I may be able to offer you the half of this wheaten loaf of my granary, and the half of the milk which is contained in this cup--milk that has been drawn this morning from the cows of my farm."

Juan ate the half of the bread and drank the frothy milk.

"Now here is my hand," he said, as he stretched out his arm, "in proof of the love and friendship which I feel for you. God grant that peace and good understanding may never become broken again between us!"

"Amen, with all my heart!" replied Roman, as he grasped the hand of John.

The solemn treaty of peace was ratified by both.

At a signal from the old men their respective huntsmen advanced, and warmly embraced each other with evident signs of joy.

While this scene was taking place, three men who were concealed in the crevices of the surrounding broken rocks were biting their lips, tossing their arms about in anger, and uttering fearful curses, in evident proof of their wrath on beholding that peace was being established between these two families, which had been so greatly divided until that moment.

When the old men with their respective escorts once more took the road to return to their houses, the three concealed men held a long conference together, and then wended their way to Pagollaga, following a most devious path. This path or road was not then what it is now. At that epoch, matted brushwood grew on the margins of the Urumea, where with difficulty a passage could be effected across the spontaneous vegetation that grew in such tangled masses. The creaking noise of the windmill did not break the silence of the wilds, nor did the puffs of the forge cast on the winds clouds of brilliant sparks. No road led to the river; no bridge existed by which to cross its waters. Nature in all her pristine splendour flung her gifts and graces on the untrod woods, on the broken rocks and hillsides, and along the bubbling fountain streams. Up the river, in the direction of the town of Arano, the Urumea formed a rude angle. The reason of this was an isolated rock or cliff which formed a kind of promontory, and spread its darksome stony branches into the centre of the river.

On the heights of this rocky promontory, that resembled the ruined tower of some castle which had been reduced to ashes during an invasion, could be seen sitting a decrepit old hag known throughout the neighbouring districts by the appellation of "the witch of Pagollaga." This sibyl was at the time engaged in peeling roots, which no doubt were to be employed for some decoction. On beholding the three men advancing towards this cliff she stopped her work. A sharp whistle was heard piercing the air. The three men who had so greatly resented the reconciliation effected between the two families then stopped in their walk, and the old woman descended from the top of the rock to join them.

Nothing could be more alike than the three who had interrupted the old woman in her task of preparing the roots. The same black, fiery eyes, the same yellow hue of countenance, mouths with coarse, red lips that barely covered the white, sharp-pointed teeth. The colour of their hair was similar; the number even of their hairs, had it been possible to count them, would have been found alike. Height, tone of voice, manner of walking--all, in one word, was so exactly alike that they had often been mistaken for each other.

On seeing the old woman, who was dressed in a green wrapper covered with red embroidery, the three men advanced a few steps to meet her.

"I was already awaiting you," said the witch, in a low, quavering voice. "Have you come for the philter?"

"Yes, we have come for it. But besides what we had ordered of you, we need a new product from your evil arts."

"Do you perchance wish to poison the girl?" she asked.

The men looked at one another in a strange way.

"Now give us the draught which is to enkindle in the heart of the girl a love for one of us."

"The draught is already prepared. But an idea has occurred to me on seeing that all you three love her with the same frenzy--what will become of the two rejected ones when she shall have chosen the one?" said the old woman.

The same strange, fierce look of theirs once more shot from the eyes of the men on hearing this question.

"That is our affair," the men replied, after they had looked at each other for a considerable time.

"Let it be so," said the witch. "But if I mistake not, I think you asked me for another beverage besides the one I have already prepared for you?

"Yes, it is so."

"What effect do you wish it to produce?

"We wish to madden the person who shall drink it," the three replied together.

Nothing easier. When I descried you coming along I was employed in peeling some roots which, on being prepared by me, will produce the desired effect."

"We shall pay you handsomely for it."

"Such is my hope. I can give you a quantity which, if properly administered, will suffice to madden one-half of the inhabitants of San Sebastian. Your idea is truly a splendid one; and I already seem to see hundreds of men, women, and children dancing about, wriggling like snakes, and uttering cries like a pack of wolves. It will indeed be a worthy scene; and I promise you that I shall not fail to preside at the feast. I repeat it--it is an excellent idea. For some good reason did your father the devil cast you into this world!"

"Do you mean to say that we are children of the evil one?

"Yes--because Satan himself told me so. He placed you three among the rushes growing on the shores of the Oria; you he called Envy, you Wrath, and you Pride. 'Some one will assuredly come and gather them,' thought your father, 'and in truth will lose nothing by this find.' And he made you so like one another that perchance he himself is unable to distinguish you."

"He of Alzate had the good fortune to find us. He treated us as his own children, and gave us other names," they replied.

"The night is approaching," said one, "and we have far to go."

"Go, then!" replied the witch.

The three men passed on. The sibyl started also behind the brothers, and the four individuals disappeared in the dark, thick wood. Half an hour later, and each of the three men could have been seen carrying in his left hand a phial containing a liquor red as the cherry, and his right hand concealed in the folds of his "capusay." They walked separated from each other by a considerable distance, but frequently looking at one another in a distrustful manner.

The witch sat down on the top of the cliff, and when she had lost sight of the three brothers in the distance she burst out in a loud peal of mocking laughter.

"Oh, arch fiend!" she cried, leaping up wildly, "now will be seen whether I cannot revenge myself upon. you; your three sons will soon bear witness of my triumph!"

II.

Gabriela had risen from her couch: smiling and blushing, she sought the oaken seat which was placed at the window. Seated on that ancient bench, she had listened to the first declaration of love, and there also had she avowed what she felt.

Gabriela was beautiful. Each day the first rays of the aurora had been reflected in her lovely eyes. The first gentle breezes of morning had joyfully hastened to play among the chestnut tresses of the maid of Guipuzcoa. The very flowers bent their supple stems as the maiden passed, as though the lily, the daisy, and the purple iris were saluting her the queen of the flowers.

The graceful damsel, after waiting seated for the coming of her lover for a considerable time, at last bent her head and leaned out of her window to listen with attentive ear to the noises of the night.

It was a dark night. The Oria, which drags its turbid waters along the ancient banks of Lasarte, Zubieta, and Usurbil, now and again utters a melancholy moan on breaking its waves against the wooden piers of the bridges. It is the wrath of the muddy river, but differs from the anger of the ocean, which at first moans, then displays its fury by terrific roars, and startles and convulses nature. The tops of the lofty oaks that cover the valley of Urnieta are also moved, and produce a noise similar to the rushing of the waters of the far distant torrents. Immense clouds of dry yellow leaves had collected together from the depths of the leafy woods, and, rising up, appeared in the night-time, to be flocks of bats and nocturnal birds, formed noisy whirlwinds, spread themselves about on the night winds, and fell on the agitated waters of the Cantabrian Sea or on the rivers.

Gabriela listened attentively to all these noises and confused rumours, that are no more than the breathing of sleepy nature. But amid all these noises the "lecayo" [2] of Antonio de Azcue, the best beloved of her heart, does not reach her ear. One hour passed away, and then another; the hermitage of Saint Barbara erected on a height like a stork's nest, begins to lose its vague outline, and becomes enveloped in a white mist, in whose centre are held mysterious meetings by beings still more mysterious. Gabriela suddenly shudders. The colour faded from her cheeks, and her countenance lost that tender smile of loving expectation, and a strange look of inquietude takes its place, caused by the delay of her lover. The far distant sound of bells begins to fill space. It is not the joyous ringing announcing a festival day; neither is it the thundering peal which proclaims a fire. The slow movement and meas-

30

ured compass of the tongues of bronze has something sad about it. Gabriela had forgotten that the first hour of the second of November had heralded the day when the Church commemorates the faithful departed. Trembling, and visibly agitated, nay, in terror, does she listen to the tolling of the bells, which now has distinctly reached her ears, and then, in a troubled, vague manner, she was about to quit the window, when she heard a sharp, piercing cry, which above the moaning of the river, the rustling of the oak, the whirl of the dry flying leaves, and the doleful tolling of the bells, caused her to shudder. That cry announced the arrival of her lover.

"On what a day and at what hour does he come to speak to me of love!" she exclaimed. "My God, protect the holy souls!"

Gabriela cast herself down on her knees to the ground. Another hour passed away, and another; yet the youth did not appear. And the river continued to moan, the oaks to sway in the night winds, the dry leaves to fly in a whirlwind, and the bells to toll.

III.

Have you ever seen in some Eastern city the sharp pointed spire of a mosque rising up in space? Have you seen on the tranquil waters of a bay the uplifted mast of a battle-ship in full array? Have you seen in the far distance, standing out in the blue horizon, the towering branches of a proud oak of the forest rising majestically above all the other trees?

Very well. The highest minaret of an Eastern mosque, the handsomest mast of a full-rigged ship on the waters, or the loveliest waving branches of the regal oak, were not more beautiful and graceful than was Antonio de Azcue. He had just finished to replenish the mangers of the curral; his aged father had repeated the prayers for the eternal repose of the soul of her who had been his loving wife; the sisters of Antonio had saluted him with a loving kiss. All things were calm and quiet in the house of Azcue.

The youth wrapped himself up in his "capusay," he grasped the knotty staff, and, closing the house door, he ran at full speed across the fields. The rough broken ascents of Goiburu did not offer any difficulties to his rapid speed; the darksome valley in which they terminated did not stop his speedy walk. In this manner was he crossing the open space upon which stands the noble town of Urnieta; swiftly, agile, and joyfully he had commenced to clamber over the stony road which leads to the gate of Arricarte. On reaching that height he could descry before him, across the darksome shades of night, the pale reflection of the murmuring waves of the Oria; to the right, the ancient hermitage of Saint Barbara; to the left, the bleak bare ridge of mountains which abruptly ends near the houses of Andoaina. Then, removing his cap and wiping his heated brow, he uttered the "lecayo," which was his lover's signal to Gabriela.

He was preparing to descend towards Lasarte, when the sad tolling of the bells reached his ears. The youth involuntarily shuddered. He remembered that his mother had died on the second of November. The agitation of Antonio, on remembering that it was "All Souls' Day" was, however, fleeting. Gabriela was waiting for him--Gabriela, whom he had not seen for a long time by reason of the feud existing between the two families, but which happily had now quite disappeared, and good relationship was established among them. Hence, stopping a few moments to say a short prayer, he soon started, brimming over with love and joy.

The path he was crossing continued for a great distance, far into the forest of ancient oaks and chestnut trees, with their huge worm-eaten trunks and spreading branches. When he entered its confines, the night was completely dark. It was necessary to grope along carefully. Suddenly a small light seemed to emerge from the centre of the aged trees, a light of an undefinable colour, a bluish-white gleam. After this it sped and appeared before the astonished gaze of the youth, who had stopped his walk on beholding this phenomena -- a shifting light which flitted about, yet without moving from the path; a light without colour or brilliancy; a light bereft of that luminous circle which radiates from other lights; a light which was not a fire gleam; a fit light for pervading a graveyard--one which could only be either enkindled or put out by the breath of the dead.

When the "Arguiduna" appears, the graves are opened, the corpses show their fleshless faces, and fling to each other this nocturnal moth, like tennis players throw with the racket the ball to one another. It is the sport of the dead during the first hours of the second of November.

On the spot where stood Antonio de Azcue, a great battle had been fought in ancient times. The youth in terror looked to the right and to the left, expecting every moment to see the ground beneath him opened, and the victims of war that are buried there rise up and show their white skulls, to come and join in this dismal festival.

But the forest and all its surroundings continued dark and silent, and the earth refused to reveal its dead. Encouraged by that silence and calm, he took heart, and continued to intern himself further into the wood.

The "Arguiduna," however, sped back, and in view of its flitting movements, which appeared to increase gradually, evidently implied that it wished to oppose the progress of the young man.

"Unhappy mother!" he cried, "you are doubtless unaware that the feuds which existed between the two families are at an end. Allow me to pass, dear mother; Gabriela is waiting for me."

Nevertheless, "Arguiduna" obstinately remained on the same spot.

Antonio, removing his cap, saluted the light, left the beaten track, and continued to walk along the brushwood. But the light also shifted, and placed itself in front of the youth, This time there was no doubt.

"I love Gabriela," he said. "I obeyed you during life, my mother; it is but just that I should respect and obey you also after death. Good-night, dear mother, good-night!"

And Antonio retired by the same way as he had come. The light followed him, and only left his presence after he had crossed the narrow valley of Goiburu.

IV.

In the meantime an extraordinary scene was taking place in the centre of the forest of chestnut trees. The branches were swaying about, moved by a mysterious power which was not due to the winds, since the wind had gone down. And noises were heard, vague and undefined, as though the trees, dowered with life, were murmuring some words; and perchance he who would believe that they spoke would not be far wrong.

The air which was breathed in that wood seemed to be impregnated with poisonous vapours; the ground exhaled a hoarse wailing; in the atmosphere something was noticed which presaged some dire calamity. And in truth, on the winds was heard like the flapping of huge wings, as though the air, agitated by these wings, had acquired the force of a sudden whirlwind, which swept in a frightful manner the chestnut plantation; the moaning of the Oria was rising and increasing in fury; the tolling of the bells became more piercing and dismal. Wailings were heard which did not belong to this world of ours; the beating together of strange bodies could be felt in space; it seemed as though the sea in all its fury was rushing to inundate the wood, wrenching up the aged chestnuts, beating down the lime bushes, and crumbling up the granite steeps with which God had surrounded it.

Then in space resounded a powerful ringing voice.

"Art thou there?" it asked.

"We are," replied the trees--so it appeared.

"Ye were vanquished once, ye cursed, cursed ones!"

"It will be the last time, my father; we have come to avenge ourselves."

"'Tis well; I deliver into your hands 'Discord,' your sister, that she may help you."

Once more the beating of wings was heard; the clouds and mist which had enveloped the hermitage of Saint Barbara were rent open, and swiftly, as though impelled by a supernatural power, they crossed the Oriamendi, passed on, grating against the promontory of Igueldo, slipped over the surface of the sea, swelling the billows, and became lost in the far distance on the uttermost limits of the dark horizon.

By degrees the wailing of the earth ceased, the swaying of the trees, the sinister noises of the air all disappeared, as though the atmosphere had become purified. Then in the dark began the mysterious dialogue which follows:

"Do each of you occupy your places?"

"Yes," replied a voice close by.

"Yes," repeated another voice, like its echo.

"Where are you, Envy?"

33

"Here I am."

At that moment two lights gleamed among the branches of a chestnut tree. They were the eyes of one of the brothers. This light was soon extinguished.

"And you Pride--where are you?

"I am here."

Two more lights gleamed like the former from the branches of a second tree, and these were the eyes of the second brother, and they also became quickly extinguished.

"And you, Wrath, my, favourite brother--where are you?"

"Here I am."

And, like to the two previous trees, two lights flashed from out a third chestnut. These three trees formed a perfect triangle; and, as before, the two lights were soon put out.

"The place, my brothers, is a capital one."

"We sought a suitable position with all care."

"Will Antonio pass this way to-night?"

"So Gabriela believes."

"And our father also."

"Then it is an arranged affair?

"Have we not already arranged it all?"

"Nevertheless, we have not decided upon the manner of effecting it."

"I vow by my axe."

"I by my arrow."

"I by my dagger."

"At length we are agreed."

"But do not agree as to the means."

"It is strange, because we have always had similar thoughts and ideas!"

"The same hatreds and the same loves!

"We three hate peace."

"All of us hate Antonio Azcue."

"All three are in love with Gabriela."

"And Gabriela in return does not love any of us."

Three red flashes shot from the branches of the ancient chestnut trees, and crossed in space.

"And the philter?"

"It is in the fountain."

"After to-morrow she will drink it."

"At the dawn------"

"That is to say, that towards night------"

"She will love one of us!"

"If in spite of all this she should persist in her dislike of us all three--what then?

"It will be worse for us."

"It will be worse for her!"

"Discord," who was listening to this dialogue, made a horrible gesture, and flapped her black wings with joy and satisfaction. Then she cautiously approached each of her brothers, whispered some words in his ear, rose up in the air, and said--

"Silence, my brothers! Your enemy will not be long coming now."

All things lapsed into silence; and, excepting the moaning of the waters of the Oria, and the measured tolling of the far distant bells, no voice or sound came to break the silence and calm of that dreadful night.

V.

The "Arguiduna" had fulfilled half its mission. Scarcely had Antonio returned home than it traced a blue line on the horizon, and then disappeared in the forest of chestnuts and oaks. And the wood continued immersed in darkness and silence.

"Arguiduna," fleeting, unquiet, like the capricious bee which flits from flower to flower, drinking the nectar enclosed in their corollas, formed moving circles around the branches of the trees. It hovered for a moment above the robust top of a chestnut, and the small reflection of Arguiduna illumined for a brief moment a human face. A sharp cry rent the air at that moment; the human face closed its eyes, a long arrow pierced from side to side that head; then was heard the gnashing of teeth, followed by a heavy fall, and lastly, a metallic, hoarse laugh.

And the little pale light, swift and unquiet like the capricious bee that hovers from flower to flower, placed itself between two gigantic trees. This time the small reflection of "Arguiduna" illumined two human faces, which were very like each other.

Two sharp cries interrupted the silence of the night; the two faces closed their gleaming eyes, long arrows pierced those two heads; then was heard terrible gnashing of teeth from both, two heavy falls, two fiendish bursts of laughter, and finally in space resounded the following words

"Rest in peace, my brothers; it is the first time that 'Discord' desires you this."

After this was heard the heavy flight of the fabulous bird, which, crossing the Oriamendi, touched the promontory of Igueldo, slid over the agitated waves of the sea, and became lost in the dark distance of the infinite. And the light, lively, brisk, and unquiet, like the capricious bee that flies from flower to flower, proceeded to poise itself on a leaf of the walnut tree which stood over the spring of limpid waters.

VI.

On the hearth in the house of Azcue crackles the fire fed by huge beech faggots. The comfortable warmth which is diffused throughout that hall also sheds a beneficent influence on the curral. This curral, or cow-house, is separated from the kitchen by a boarding, along which runs a manger, and above are long slits or grating, through which are seen the cattle when housed for the night. From the walls are suspended bundles of arrows, polished bows, racks of arms, hatchets, hoes, and implements and weapons of all descriptions. In a word, all kinds of arms which symbolize warfare, and implements of agriculture that are emblems of peace.

Juan de Azcue is reciting the Litanies; his daughters reply in chorus without ceasing from their work, and directing from time to time anxious though tender glances toward their brother Antonio, who, sad and pensive, replies mechanically to the family prayers.

The cattle show their horned heads across the open spaces of the kitchen partition, and glance around with their large, soft eyes now on Antonio, now on his sisters, as though they would wish to ask an explanation for the sadness of the one and of the loving solicitude of the latter. The mobile, elastic muzzle of the cows move, as though they also were murmuring a response to the litany of the patriarch of the family; the bells hanging around their necks remain quiet and dumb. To this calm scene is added a touch of sweet sadness by the cooing of a dove which is heard at intervals. A simple yet sympathetic challenge; a token of a pure, constant love.

Nevertheless a form is wanting to complete that family picture--the form of greatest interest. Among that group of maidens is not seen the form of the mother. In that group is wanting the being all abnegation, all love, the greatest emanation of the love of God; because nothing approaches so nearly to Divine love as the love of the mother. The seat she usually occupied is now vacant; that seat no one dares to fill; it is a sacred thing, which will be religiously respected from age to age.

Eight o'clock has struck; the patriarch has finished his prayer; he blesses his family, and slowly retires to his chamber. As soon as the old man left the room, the young women rose up and surrounded the young man, who was sadly caressing the cooing dove. One sister flung her arms around the neck of the beloved brother; another leaned over the back of his chair and touched his brow with her lips; a third stood before him with folded arms silently watching him; whilst a fourth put her hands under his chin and made him lift up his face. A charming group, worthy of the brush of a Michael Angelo!

"From what proceeds this sadness, dear brother?" they lovingly asked. "Did not Gabriela receive you last night? Did she perchance tell you some bad news? Is there any obstacle to mar your happiness? Answer us, dear brother, answer us."

"Last night I saw our mother in the chestnut plantation of Arricarte," replied the young man.

The group of women gave a sudden start, and the girls, pale with terror, and eyes streaming with tears, repeated in a low voice:

"Did you see our mother?"

"Yes, my sisters, and she opposed the way, that I might not go to where love was calling me."

"Is it possible?" they cried in one voice.

"Yes; listen how this happened. You know that a mother does not only love her children while she remains in the world, but even from the next world she still encircles them with her love, and watches over them with tenderness and solicitude, so that no harm should befall them."

"It is true," replied the maidens, unconsciously approaching to their brother.

"You also know that of all mothers, ours was the best."

"That is very true," replied the girls.

"I was walking lightly and swiftly, full of joy, because peace had been established between the family of Alzate and ours, and been solemnly ratified. On reaching the wood, the 'Arguiduna' appeared before me. I saluted her lovingly, judging that it was the spirit of our beloved mother. The 'Arguiduna' never departed from the path. I retired from the track of the beaten path," continued the youth, "and decided to walk along the brushwood. The 'Arguiduna' turned also and stood before me!"

"Ah! some evil was threatening you, my brother," said the youngest sister.

"Perhaps so, Juana, perhaps so."

"This is quite certain. When the 'Arguiduna' places itself before any one, it is to warn him of some danger which lies before him, should he not turn back."

"I obeyed the order she gave me. I returned home, followed by the light, which only left me when I had traversed the marsh of Goiburu."

"Do not doubt it, Antonio, our good mother has saved you from some grave danger."

"Or else she has wished to save me from some great affliction, Beatrice," murmured the youth.

"Oh, good gracious!" they all cried in one voice, "do you think------"

"I know that I dearly love Gabriela, my sisters, and also am aware that I am hapless!"

"My brother! do not depreciate one who will so soon be our sister. Gabriela has sworn love to you; and Gabriela, like a true Guipuzcoan, will never be wanting to her vows."

"I shall know that to-night," replied Antonio, rising up. "I shall go to Alzate, and will cross the chestnut plantation; I shall see Gabriela, so good-night, my sisters, good-night."

"May the Lord guide you on your way, and may our good mother defend you, my brother!" reverently replied the young damsels.

An hour later, Antonio de Azcue was uttering his sharp "lecayo," which awakened the echoes of the mountains.

VII.

Antonio began to descend quickly the mountain, and entered the plantation. The last hours of the second day of November had not yet struck. The chestnut wood was enveloped in darkness--intensely dark. A sepulchral silence reigned throughout space, in strange contrast to what had occurred on the previous night. No sound crossed its leafy luxuriance, the branches of the huge trees remained motionless; even the moaning of the Oria had subsided, and its waters seemed to have lost their power; the bronze tongues of the bells hung silent within their concave hollows; not even a breath of air stirred the dry leaves which covered the ground.

Suddenly, as on the previous evening, he saw among the moss-covered trunks of the trees the same pale light of undefinable colour, bluish-white. But on this occasion the light was behind him; he turned his face, and noticed that the "Arguiduna" was following him at about two yards' distance.

"Good-night, my mother, good-night," said Antonio, saluting and uncovering his head. "This night we have prayed longer for the eternal repose of your soul."

The gleam of light visibly twinkled, and for a brief moment shed a more vivid reflection around.

"Pass on before me, mother; your son desires that you should guide him after death across the dark path of life, in the same way as you guided him when you lived."

But the light twinkled more then ever, then approached the youth, yet kept behind him. Antonio continued walking, followed by the "Arguiduna." He had reached the densest part of the wood, when he noticed that the pale light which had illumined his path was gradually diminishing its intensity; he turned quickly round, fearing lest the light should disappear altogether before he had time to bid it a loving farewell; but a horrible scene presented itself to his view. Three livid heads with rough matted hair and wild glassy eyes occupied a small opening in the wood, and formed a triangle. On the forehead of one was written in red characters the word "Pride," on the next the word "Wrath," and upon the third, "Envy." Sharp arrows pierced through their foreheads, and a fearful expression of pain and rage contracted the muscles of those three blood-stained heads. The flickering light had poised itself in the centre of the triangle of heads "Pride" then curled its vicious mouth and blew. "Arguiduna" swiftly flew until it touched the red lips of the head upon the brow of which was written the word "Wrath." This one also blew at the light, and the colourless flame flew away and stumbled against "Envy." This game was very rapid. The light faded by moments; its swift movements lessened visibly, the volume of its bluish flame was fast weakening.

The heads meanwhile, without losing the contraction of features produced by acute pain, laughed in a mute manner, nervously and inwardly, and formed a frightful contrast to the visible suffering which could be remarked on their drawn faces. And the light faded more and more, its movements slower, its flame grew sensibly smaller.

"Arguiduna" appeared to suffer acutely; "Arguiduna" was asking assistance in its own mysterious language; it was evidently wrestling with those inexorable heads, which were redoubling their puffs on beholding and enjoying the sufferings of the little flame. The light was now almost extinguished; the laughter of those three heads became more frightfully significative.

"My mother! my dearest mother!" cried Antonio in despairing accents, as he flew towards the open space.

The three heads suddenly turned round towards the young man. Their glassy eyes were darting undefinable flames of wrath. The light flickered once--took form, and swift as thought leaped over the space occupied by the three heads, and came to place itself at the feet of Antonio, casting around a luminous resplendency.

A noise and rumble similar to that which nature will utter at the moment of its complete destruction shook the neighbouring mountains to their very foundations. The Oria stopped its course; the bell-tower shook and broke out in dismal tolling; the waves of the Cantabrian Sea stayed its rapid threatening march. Antonio looked towards the open space. The three heads had disappeared. The "Arguiduna" was moving gracefully, and displayed its relief and joy by shedding around soft yet bright beams.

*   *   *   *   *   *

Since that memorable night, never was "Discord" seen again in the Guipuzcoan territory. From that night also the three evil creatures, Pride, Wrath, and Envy, are unknown on that noble soil.

On the following morning, Gabriela and Antonio left the house of Alzate together, and bent their steps towards the fountain spring over which towers the walnut tree.

The two lovers, on approaching to drink of its waters, noticed a strange thing. The pure water of the spring was tinged with a red colour. The philter of the "witch of Pagollaga" was mixed in its streams. In course of time, whenever Antonio crossed the chestnut plantation of Arricarte, the "Arguiduna," swift, joyful, like the capricious bee that flits from flower to flower, would always accompany him with watchful solicitude and care, flickering brightly and casting around brilliant resplendencies, and then the youthful heir of Azcue would lovingly say to it:

"My dearest mother, Gabriela and prayed last night fervently for the eternal repose of your soul. Gabriela and I love you tenderly, and we shall teach our children to love you also most lovingly, even as we do."

[1] Fatuous fire, or *Will-o'-the-Wisp*."
[2] Lecayo--a cry of joy which is used as a signal.

Maitagarri

[1]

I. ITURRIOZ.

[2]

THE most profound silence reigned in one of the houses of the suburbs of Oyarzun. Pedro Iturrioz, the head of the family, a robust mountaineer of advanced age, had finished his supper; and his wife some years younger than he, was at his side offering him a cup of warm wine, and awaited that her husband should address her. The chieftain made a sign, and the wife placed in his hands a silver cup with a gesture of tender love and deep respect. She then laid on the table a basket filled with luscious fruit, and sat down at the further end of the room at her wheel, spinning the finest thread, which later on would become converted into handkerchiefs, towels, and perfumed linen, such as abounds in quantities in all Basque homes. At another corner of the kitchen, two girls of singular beauty, were conversing in a low tone with a youth of about fifteen years of age who stood with uncovered head.

A long settle, ornamented with large brass nails, could be seen unoccupied beneath the wide chimney roof, to the right of the hearth. The gleams from the crackling fire on the hearth, and the bright rays of a flambeau of hempen cord and rosin which hung from an iron ring, lit up this family group. The chief divided a beautiful apple and gave one half to his wife, then drank two-thirds of the warm wine in the cup, and invited her to finish the rest; this she did without saying a word. The mountaineer then uncovered his venerable head, and all rose up on seeing this action. He made the sign of the cross, murmured a prayer in which all present joined, and then sat down on the settle by the fireside.

One of the girls removed the supper things, carefully folded the white cloth, and then all the family sat clown around the fire. The mistress of the house was spinning, the young girls were winding skeins of thread on wooden reels, the youth sharpened a woodman's knife, meanwhile that Pedro Iturrioz, leaning his elbow on the arms of the settle, appeared lost in thought. The eyes of all were directed to the countenance of the old man, whose eyes were gradually closing in sleep. The wife made quietly a sign; the conversation of the girls ceased, and the young man intoned in a low voice a simple monotonous song, the cadences of which were marked by the three women moving their hands. The melody certainly acted with much power on the aged man, for his head fell over his breast in deep sleep.

Through the half-open door poured in the beams of the moon, which was illuminating the magnificent landscape of luxuriant trees and gigantic mountains; the ripple of the mountain stream was also heard, imparting on that quiet scene a singular charm. For a length of time did all things remain in this way, until suddenly the old man awoke and said:

"Tell me, Antonio, what did you hear on the mountain?"

The youth threw down. the knife which he was sharpening, rose up, and respectfully replied:

"I heard, father, that the battle proved a bloody one."

"Do you know who were the vanquished?"

"I was not told, father.""

The old man remained silent. The eldest girl turned deadly pale, and allowed the skein she was winding to fall to the ground, and gazed on her brother as though she wished to interrogate him with her looks. Antonio, however, awaited his father's permission to speak.

"To-morrow, ere it is light, proceed to the frontier, and do not return until you learn what success the combat has had," said the father.

"I will do so," replied the youth.

"Then approach nearer to me and listen, Antonio."

"What do you wish me to do?" Antonio asked, bending down his ear to listen to the words his father desired to speak confidentially.

"Gil is with them," he said, in a deeply moved voice; "he is your brother and my son, ask, explore the camp and when you return tell me that you saw him alive, or, else, if he is dead, that you buried him in a Christian manner."

"I will comply with your orders, father."

"Should he be living, tell him from me that I forbid him--do you understand? I forbid him to use his weapons against those of Arpide so long as they are before the enemy," continued the father.

"And to me, do you also forbid me this?"

"Yes, my son. Feuds and private resentments, although they may lie deep, should be hushed and laid aside when it is a question of saving the country. Cursed may he be who shall do otherwise."

The old man rose up, kissed the foreheads of the three women, blessed Antonio, and slowly quitted the kitchen. Half an hour later he was sleeping the calm sleep of the just man.

Scarcely had Pedro Iturrioz left the room than the women surrounded Antonio.

"Your father has communicated to you secret commands which are not given to me to know," said the mother, with saintly resignation. "Obey him, my son, implicitly; your father holds the place of God in this world."

"This you have always taught me, my mother," replied the youth, kissing her.

"So it is, Antonio, but after the father it appertains to the mother to counsel her children. Sit down and listen to me."

The three young people sat down, the mother between her two daughters, one of which betrayed considerable anguish, While the other was lovingly watching her. Antonio knelt before Catalina and fixed his black eyes upon her. The wife of Iturrioz was caressingly playing with the curly locks of her son.

"Antonio," she said, "your brother is fighting on the frontier. You well know his fiery character: if he still lives, tell him to fulfil his duty like the brave;

nevertheless, not to attempt or risk his life in senseless, heedless undertakings."

"I will tell him so," replied the youthful Antonio.

"Tell him," continued Catalina, "that he is to forget our private questions, and only remember that he is a Guipuzcoan, and that his enemies are those who are enemies to the country."

"My brother, do not forget these prudent counsels," interrupted the maiden, who was evidently suffering grief.

"What do you know of these affairs, Inez?" demanded Antonio, giving her a searching look.

"It is true," replied the girl, blushing, "that I understand but little about these things, but I nevertheless believe that sound reason dictates these counsels."

"My mother, what you have just advised me is the same as my father bade me do."

"God be praised!" replied Catalina. "Now nothing else remains to advise, but that you are not to linger on the journey. Receive your mother's blessing, and may God protect your brothers! My girls, let us retire."

They all rose up and left the kitchen. The household remained only under the protection of the laws of the country, and watched and guarded by a mastiff which stretched itself before the fire.

II. THE WITCH OF ZALDIN

The hour of midnight was striking when the outer door of the house was slowly opened, and an aged woman entered the kitchen. The mastiff lifted up his head, uttered a growl, approached the new comer, and then, turned lazily to lie down again. The woman threw some dry branches on the fire, and a brilliant flame lit up the hospitable room. After this she imitated to perfection the screech of an owl, and a light step was very soon after heard descending the stairs from the first floor. Dominica, the youngest of the daughters of Pedro Iturrioz, had just entered, and stopped at some distance, looking at the stranger with a look of fear and respect depicted on her countenance.

"Approach, Dominica, and come and sit by my side," said the old woman.

The maiden obeyed, and sat on the wooden bench occupied by her interlocutor; the mastiff then rose and lay at the feet of Dominica, placing his intelligent head between her knees. That group, lit up by the firelight, and standing out in relief against the blackened walls, partook somewhat of the weird character of witchcraft. The old woman with her brown wrinkled brow, round, unquiet eyes, red tangled hair, and long pointed nose, formed a strange contrast to the fresh checks, beautiful, expressive black eyes, lithe waist, and graceful smile of Dominica. To complete the picture, we will add that the old woman drew her face close to the fair countenance of the maiden, the mastiff meanwhile watching with his penetrative sight all the movements of the witch.

"Did you send for me, Dominica?" asked the old woman, in a low voice. "Well, here I am: what do you want with me?"

"I wished to know," replied the girl, in an agitated voice, "who were the vanquished in the battle fought on the frontier?"

"Nothing else?" questioned the witch, meanwhile attentively watching Dominica.

"Nothing more," replied the maiden, lowering her eyes.

"Very well. Open that window which looks in the direction of the camp."

"It is open," she said, throwing it back.

"Look up to the sky."

"I am looking."

"What do you see towards the west?"

"I see a grey cloud."

"What form has it taken?"

"It appears to me to be like the skeleton of a gigantic horse."

"What more do you observe?"

"I see the cloud divided in two."

"Which side is the larger half?"

"The side of the head."

"The Navarrese and the French are vanquished!" replied the witch.

Dominica gave a cry of joy, and, approaching the witch, said, "Is this certain what you tell me?

"As certain as that I am standing here. Do you wish to know more?"

"I would much like to know what has been the fate of my brother," the girl replied.

"I will satisfy your curiosity. Come near that caldron."

Dominica hastened to do as she was bidden.

"Put it on the fire, and go to the fields and bring me the roots of the plant 'virtude.'"

The girl left the house to seek the desired roots, followed by the mastiff. Then the wily pythoness drew from her pocket a leathern bag and took out of it a bundle of rags. She began to unfold most carefully this bundle until she discovered the hand of a child [3] in perfect preservation, and around this little hand were some curls of silky, golden hair. Out of a small earthenware bottle she poured some drops of red liquor into the caldron, which was already becoming hot over the fire, and waited for the return of Dominica.

She had not long to wait. The maiden soon returned, bearing a bundle of roots in her hand, and when she went near the old woman she noticed that the mastiff was pulling at her dress.

"Be quiet, Moor, be quiet," she said to the dog. "It seems you like to amuse yourself out in the moonlight!"

She then turned to the woman and gave her the roots.

"Did you gather these roots under the shadow?" the old witch asked, as she took them from Dominica.

"Yes, under the shadow of a walnut tree."

"It is well; sit down on the bench and watch with all attention the caldron."

The witch threw the carefully peeled roots into the cauldron, the contents of which were beginning to boil. A few moments after there rose up a blue flame, which cast a weird reflection on the furniture of the kitchen.

"What do you see?" inquired the witch.

"I see my brother covered with blood and sleeping calmly. I see many dead lying on the battle-field. Ah me!" she cried, suddenly.

"What more do you see?"

"I see Juan de Arpide also sleeping at some distance. There are many camp fires; I see sentinels."

"Look towards your brother; what is he doing?"

"Good heavens!" cried Dominica, turning pale.

"What is taking place?" asked the witch.

"My brother rises up, unsheathes his sword, and cautiously approaches Juan de Arpide."

Your brother and Arpide must fight, and blood will flow," said the witch, in a woeful tone of voice. "What more do you see?"

"Nothing more," replied Dominica, trembling.

"Turn your face towards the wall," continued the witch; "attentively observe the figures which will be depicted on the wall."

Dominica obeyed, and, uttering a cry of anguish, she covered her eyes with her hands.

"It is impossible for me to look," the girl said, greatly agitated.

"Take your hands from your face and tell me what you see; I have no time to listen to your cries and sobs."

"I see Juan de Arpide, and a woman is holding him up in her arms."

"Do you know that woman?

"Her face is turned away from me."

"Look attentively towards Arpide; what is his colour?"

He is pale, very pale."

Are you satisfied?" asked the witch, with an evil smile on her wrinkled face.

"My poor sister!" exclaimed Dominica, weeping.

"Your brother has shed the blood of the lover of Inez. Do you wish to know further about these love affairs?"

The mastiff howled and placed its two paws on the shoulders of the maiden, and licked her face.

"Good gracious!" murmured Dominica.

"Make up your mind quickly; they are waiting for me elsewhere these last two hours."

The girl hesitated, while the dog, continued to lick its young mistress's face, meanwhile eyeing savagely the old woman.

44

"Bah! you are weak-spirited," then said the witch, putting her bag away and preparing to depart.

"Wait! stay a moment!" Dominica cried, as she pulled at the dress of the old woman to detain her.

"I cannot remain longer in this house," replied the old woman, looking askance at the mastiff.

"Very well, then I decide," said the girl.

The dog gave a piteous whine, and, leaving the girl, went to a corner and rolled itself up.

"Take this bag, now that you have made up your mind to do as you are bid, and observe anew the blue flame."

"I will do so," said Dominica, taking the bag, and making a great effort to overcome her fear.

"Open the bag, and throw into the caldron one by one all the objects it contains."

Dominica obeyed; but when she drew forth the mutilated member, and saw it in her hand, enwrapped with a curl of hair, she felt such a sensation of horror that she threw it, the bag and all its contents, into the fire which burned on the hearth.

A fearful detonation shook the house, and when the girl wished to fly away she could not. Her knees bent under her, and she fell to the ground, uttering a piercing cry. She saw the "witch of Zaldin" cast herself forth out of the window, transformed into a monstrous bat.

The fire slowly became extinguished, and the room remained in total darkness.

III. THE AVOWAL

It was at break of day when Antonio, dressing hurriedly, prepared to leave the house. At the door he was met by Inez, seated on the doorstep, breathing nervously the fresh morning breeze.

"Good morning, Inez," he said, kissing her on the forehead. "Why have you risen so early?"

"I wished to see you before you left the house."

"Thank you, my Inez; in this I know your love for me. Why is not Dominica with you?"

"She is asleep, I suppose. But listen, Antonio: I am alone because I wished to confer with you. You are young, I know, but nevertheless the counsels of men of your age are more prudent and just than those of women at mine."

Antonio looked at his sister, and noticed by the light of the dawn that she was very pale.

"Are you ill, my sister?" he affectionately asked.

"Yes, Antonio, sick in body, and more so in the soul."

"Poor Inez! what can I do for you? Speak, for you well know that I love you tenderly."

Inez raised her eyes and fixed them in such a searching manner on her brother, that he felt deeply wounded.

"Do you perchance doubt my affection?" he asked.

"Such a doubt on your part would wound me much."

"Far from it, my brother," sweetly replied Inez: "I am going to confide to you something which is unknown to Gil or to our father."

"That will comfort me," replied Antonio, sitting close to her.

"The hours are passing swiftly, my brother, and you have far to go; listen to me, therefore, and be indulgent to me."

"Speak, Inez, speak. I will listen attentively."

Inez took the hand of Antonio between hers, and began her narrative in the following way:

"You are aware of the fearful enmity which exists between our family and that of Arpide: this enmity is the principal cause of my unhappiness."

"Why so?" asked Antonio, in a tone of fear.

"Because the case is this, my brother. I have met Juan, and the first time I saw him I flew from his presence."

"You did well, my sister. The injury his father did to our father is unpardonable."

"Listen to me to the end. From that day he never ceased to follow me. If I went to Oyarzun to church, accompanied by my mother, I was certain to meet him at the church door; he would kneel close to us during Mass, and when we left the temple we used to find him at the porch. When we returned home he always followed us at a distance."

"Without addressing a word to you?"

"He never dared to do so. When I approached to my window I could always see him, with bow slung on shoulder, standing on the summit of the mountain, his eyes fixed on our house."

"Perchance does that man harbour any evil designs against us?"

"No!" quickly replied Inez. "The spring came, and at daydawn, when I used to open the window of my room, I always found each morning a crown of flowers on the sill. At first I used to throw the flowers to the ground, because I felt certain that he would be concealed somewhere in the wood, and watching what I did. But on the following day I would meet Juan, either in the woods or close to the fountain; and on his countenance there was such a look of deep sadness that I could not help pitying him."

Antonio withdrew his hand from that of his sister's and remained pensive.

"Listen to me, brother, for pity's sake. His reserve and respectful conduct arrested my attention in an extraordinary manner; I thought of him more frequently than I should, and in spite of every effort I made to drive his image from my mind, I found it impossible to do so....It was at the twilight hour; I was returning from visiting the dead remains of our poor Cousin Lucia, whom we all so dearly loved; it began to snow heavily, and the road was impassable. On reaching the cross which stands close to the spring, I saw a black form standing in the middle of the road; this form had eyes which were flashing in the darkness like two flames, and fixed on me; I grew so alarmed that I remained rooted to the spot; nor could I even cry out. The form gave a terrific howl, and cast itself on me."

"Perhaps it was Juan?" exclaimed the lad, leaping to his feet. "Wretch!"

"No, my brother, it was not he. It was the dreadful wolf, the terror of all the district------"

"The one which was found dead close to the fountain?"

"Poor sister!" he said, taking once more the hand of his sister.

"My death was certain," she continued, shuddering. "When I beheld the animal close upon me, grinding his teeth and howling, the excess of fear made me utter a piercing scream, and just as I was about to fall a prey to the clutches of the wolf, I saw a human form emerge from the far end of the road, place itself between the beast and myself, and receive the first encounter. The two then wrestled in a desperate manner; and what added to the horror of the moment was the fact that neither the wolf howled, nor did the man who fought with it utter a cry; it was a dumb encounter, yet a fierce one. What I endured at that moment is simply indescribable. I believed in good faith that the man who thus wrestled with the beast was Gil."

During the narrative of this encounter, Antonio pressed convulsively the hands of Inez.

"The combat continued for nearly ten minutes," continued the maiden. "The wolf fell down dead, strangled by the iron grip of my liberator. He then approached me, and you may judge what my surprise must have been when I recognized in him Juan de Arpide------"

"Juan de Arpide!" cried Antonio, in deep astonishment.

"Yes, my brother, I owe him my life. He besought me to allow him to see me home, and to swear to him never to tell any one what had taken place. I gave the desired promise, and until to-day I have kept my oath."

"And have you seen him since?" asked, Antonio.

"Many times, my brother; because from that moment I found it impossible to keep from loving him."

Saying this, she blushed and hid her face on the breast of her brother. The youth felt greatly moved on hearing this tender avowal.

"Do you know, Inez," Antonio asked, after a moment's pause--"do you know whether he loves you?"

"His lips have never told me his love; but his eyes often do. Garlands of flowers adorn my window every morning, and on the eve of his departure to fight against the enemy of our country, instead of finding the usual crown, I found only two flowers, an everlasting flower and a pansy twined together."

"His behaviour has been a truly noble one," said the youth, in a solemn tone. "Rise up, poor sister Inez lift up that brow pure as the first thought of a babe rise up, my sister; I, your brother, will protect you against all others. Should our father yield to the impulses of hatred and curse your love, and should our eldest brother do the same, I who know what has passed will never desist from protecting you, my sister. When Gil and my father shall come to know what I do, I have no doubt but they will bless you as the peacemaker

between the two families, which never ought to have been severed; they will bless you, Inez, as I bless you.

Inez threw herself into the arms of her brother, who warmly embraced her and covered her face with kisses.

"I did well to confide in you, my brother!" she cried, shedding tears of joy.

"Yes, my sister, you did well; I cannot forget that you have loved me with singular affection, and although I partake somewhat of the disposition of my father, and respect his opinion, nevertheless my heart tells me that in this respect his ideas are not the most desirable ones. Retire now, dear Inez, and await my return. Who knows what may take place?"

"Let us trust in God, my brother."

"So be it, let us trust all things to God."

"And that He may keep you in His holy keeping, dear Antonio."

They once more embraced each other, and the young man started to carry out the orders given to him by his father.

IV. THE DUEL

Along the western skirt of the hills which form a ridge from Leiza to the shores of the ocean, a horseman arrayed in armour might be seen riding along mounted on a fiery steed. From the dilapidated state of his armour, his crushed war helmet, the rusty broken cuirass, the want of feathers in the tuft worn on his casque, could be inferred that the brave knight was returning from some tournament or fierce combat. He rode on alone, without page or shield-bearer, stopping now and again to reconnoitre the country through which he passed, grasping the hilt of his sword whenever the slightest noise reached his ears, or unfastening the war hatchet which he carried suspended from the pommel of his saddle whenever a shepherd or traveller crossed his path. He left on his right the town of Goizueta; he followed the path of Urumea towards the immediate boundary of the stronghold of Articuza, a celebrated arsenal of those parts, close to which is seen a sumptuous building, the admiration of all who frequent those fastnesses. However, in those days nothing of this existed, and the very narrow valley wherein the palace and arsenal were constructed was then the wildest place in all that district.

When the horseman reached the summit of one of the mountains which surrounded that valley, the sun was setting behind the sea, and could only be descried from that spot by a golden line along the horizon far away. The knight stood still for a moment to gaze upon the scene, and then continued his journey, descending into the dark valley. On reaching near one of the broken rocks which intercepts the flow of the stream that passes at the bottom of the valley, he stopped, dismounted, and threw himself on the grass, leaving his horse to graze quietly, and prepared to enjoy a few moments of repose. But when the horseman rose to continue his march, the horse suddenly gave a loud neigh, which was quickly replied to by another. The knight leaped on his steed. and prepared himself for the defensive, expecting to be taken by surprise. He listened for some time, and it was not long before he heard the noise of hoofs trampling, and the rattle of armour. The darkness of night prevented him from distinguishing objects even at a short distance, so that it was not until the two horsemen found themselves face to face that they were able to see one another.

"Who goes there?" asked the first arrival.

"And who are you to ask me?" replied the other,

"I am a knight," said the first.

"Guipuzcoan, or Navarrese?"

"Guipuzcoan," was the reply.

"God assist you. In that case we are friends."

Saying this, they approached nearer to one another, and asked, "Where are you going to?

"Towards Oyarzun."

"Are you of that place?"

"Very near it."

"In that case your name must be well known. What may it be?"

"Juan de Arpide."

"And I am Gil de Iturrioz," replied the second.

A moment's silence followed this declaration. The two confronted each other, the first-born of each of those two families, whose feuds dated from long years.

"We meet at last on neutral ground," said Gil to his antagonist; "here we have not our arms tied through respect for the laws of the country, neither have we here to forget our private feuds in order to combat against the common enemy."

"You say well," replied Arpide, in a sad tone; "nevertheless I do not see the reason why we should measure swords when there exists no reason for rancour between us."

"Why not?" asked Gil; "does Juan de Arpide forget that his father insulted mine, or does he think that an injury done to the chieftain of the family does not bind his descendants to vengeance? A graceful inheritance it would certainly be!"

"Listen to me, Gil," replied Arpide. "I do not deny that there have existed misunderstandings in both families since the day when my father refused the hand of his sister after he had promised it, nevertheless previous to this unfortunate occurrence I have understood that there existed a close friendship between the families. Very well, must the remembrance of the good feeling be altogether extinguished by the recollection of an injury due, perhaps, to the unbridled fiery character of our parents? Let us be just, Gil; the peace which our elders severed, let us bind once more together; let us end our feuds, Gil; let us be brothers; there are over many enemies to fight with us on the plains of our country without weakening ourselves by intestine wrestling."

"By my faith, but you ought to fling down your armour and substitute the soutane," said Gil, with an ironical smile. "I can assure you that you resemble a missionary preacher more than a knight who wears spurs."

"Gil! I do not deserve this provocation on your part. You are well aware that it is not fear which induces me to speak in this way, but the desire that a good understanding and harmony should exist between us."

"On my part I do neither desire nor contemn it.. When I was born these hatreds existed between the families of Arpide and of Iturrioz; with these feuds I was brought up, and with them I shall die!"

"How wrong you do!" exclaimed Juan, in a desponding tone.

"That is not your affair," haughtily replied Gil. "In any case it does not devolve on you to counsel me, neither do I humble myself to ask your advice."

"I have not attempted to become your counsellor. You may foster your hatred as long as you wish, and may God grant it may be for a short term; but let us separate at least without using our weapons."

"You are very prudent and discreet, Arpide," said Gil, laughing. "Perchance you are more than prudent--you are a coward."

"Eight days have not yet elapsed since you yourself saw to the contrary," replied Arpide, making a great effort to restrain his anger.

"That is true; but, nevertheless, I believe that it is not the same thing to fight against common soldiers and French invaders as it is to fight against a son of Pedro Iturrioz."

"That is not the reason why I feel a repugnance to fight with you; you are well aware that I do not fear you."

"What, then, can be your motive?

"I fear the consequences which will result from this duel. God guard you, Gil; I declare that I do not wish to fight against you."

On concluding these words he set spurs to his horse and turned away.

"You do not wish it?" cried Iturrioz, in wrathful tones. "Then I will compel you to fight."

And, running up to him, he dealt a fierce blow with his mailed gauntlet at the face of Juan de Arpide.

The latter stopped, looked at Gil, dismounted and drew his sword. Gil Iturrioz did the same, and both prepared for the combat.

The spot in which they were to combat could not certainly be less fitted for fighting. The surface of the ground was scarcely level for the space of two yards; on three sides it was surrounded by dense tangled briars and brushwood, on the fourth was a fearful chasm. The night was dark, and some drops of rain were falling. The first to assault was Gil de Iturrioz, whose sword fell heavily on the shoulder of Juan de Arpide. The duel began. The broken rocks and hollow places echoed the clashing of the weapons; rays of lightning flashed at intervals from the summit of the cliff, illuminating for brief moments the armour of the combatants, and by the aid of this uncertain light it could be perceived that Gil retained the fiery gleams of his eyes, and that he struck furiously, meanwhile that the countenance of Juan revealed an expression of intense sorrow, and he only maintained an attitude of defence. The combat continued; no other sound was heard in those solitudes but the rough clanging of arms, no voice broke the stillness--not a single word did they pronounce. Any one who perchance had passed the vicinity would have judged that he was witnessing some gigantic wrestling between the spirits of darkness.

Suddenly a heavy fall was heard, and a voice which said, "Rise up, Gil, and let this end the duel."

"No, by my faith! Although you might have killed me while I lay on the ground."

"Nevertheless I did not do so. Let us, therefore finish at this point, and each go his way."

As an only reply to this was heard anew the clashing of weapons, to indicate that the fight was being continued. This did not, however, last long. A terrible blow was dealt, a cry of pain was heard, and then all things lapsed into deep silence.

Amid the shadows of the trees was seen gliding away a large form, and along the stony road was heard the tread of a horse galloping at full speed.

V. MAITAGARRI

[4]

At nightfall an the following day, Juan de Arpide found himself sitting in the most concealed part of the valley of Articuza; near him, and at the foot of a broken rock, his war-horse was quietly grazing; he felt his limbs so benumbed that he could not move. He began to recall all the events which had taken place on the previous day, and then rose to his memory the encounter he had had with Gil; his conversation with him, the duel which had followed, and its ending. He looked up towards the rock, at the base of which he was sitting, and noticed that it was on its heights that he had fought on the previous night. He then comprehended the cause of his benumbed state, and the deep holes of his broken armour told the rest. He felt bruised all over; his neck was wounded, and he was almost inanimate from want of food, since he had not taken any nourishment for some thirty hours. All human help seemed to him impossible in that solitary spot. A canopy of verdure during summer covers this wild part. The trees, with their enormous growth and extended branches, entwined with each other, and scarcely permitted the sunbeams to pierce through. The stream of pure water which flows along the base of this narrow valley bathes the trunks of the trees, and preserves a delightful freshness around. The vegetation there is strong, magnificent; and nothing more poetic can be imagined than a walk by moonlight across that calm solitude. This rivulet in places forms little lakes calm and still; small lagoons surrounded by reeds, briars, lilies, and wild roses. When gazing on the tranquil waters of these lakes in miniature, one would almost believe that he were gazing on a large mirror surrounded by flowers. Perchance some kingfisher of emeraldine hues is heard screeching, or skimming with its wings the surface of the lake; some stag quenches its thirst from the currents which feed the stream, or a nightingale perched on the branches singing plaintively, or a dove whose sad cooing invites to meditation, are the only creatures which give life to the romantic landscape.

Juan de Arpide, seeing that the night was closing in, and feeling that it would be impossible to bear the pangs of hunger until morning, called his horse, which was grazing near him, and the faithful animal soon joyously neighed in response to its master's call and came to him. After several vain attempts to mount him, he at length succeeded, and proceeded on his march. Juan found himself on the margin of one of the tiny lakes which we have just described, at the base of the cliff, from the summit of which he had rolled over on the previous night. From the middle of this lake rose a diaphanous vapour; long stems of climbing plants hung from the broken edges of the overhanging rocks, until they dipped their ends in the waters of the lake. These were covered with leaves, and formed hanging curtains similar to the reed lattices which shade Chinese windows. Long pointed reedmace grew on the margins, and the branches of a weeping willow waved at the mercy of a gentle breeze, like the feathers on a war helmet. The horseman fancied he perceived, amid the shades of night, a sudden undulation on the waters; he thought also that the overhanging stems of the climbing plants were separating; he saw the branches of the willow tree moving in a strange manner, and at last he heard the sounds of far distant melody, the mysterious echoes of which seemed to enrapture his spirit. The crystalline surface of the waters became divided, and, enveloped in the mist which rose from the lake, he saw appearing a number of maidens of incomparable beauty. Their brows were encircled by roses, and their aerial bodies were covered with robes of white gauze. Stars of pale light adorned the centre of their diadems.

They rose up softly above the surface of the water, and, taking one another's hands, the maidens began to intone the strange peculiar music which had so enthralled the attention of the horseman. All their faces were pale; their eyes were half closed and veiled by long eyelashes, their abundant hair hung down loosely over their alabaster shoulders.

Soon after this singular apparition the maidens proceeded to the spot where the knight, completely abstracted with this vision, was gazing on, and they surrounded him on all sides. One held the bridle of his horse, which seemed to be spell-bound, so quiet and motionless had the animal become; another held the stirrups so that the warrior might dismount; others removed his mailed armour; others, again, took his shield and the heavy lance; and in this state, disarmed and confused in mind on beholding himself served and waited upon by a bevy of such lovely, maidens, he allowed himself to be conducted beneath the hanging branches of the willow tree. This tree, with its waving overhanging branches, covered the entrance to a cave whose floor, carpeted with fine yellow sand, was the entrance to the magic mansion of the Maitagarri of the Pyrenees. All whatsoever the most poetic imagination of the East could invent of marvels was found collected together in the vast saloon where the maidens conducted the knight. The vaulted dome shone as though it were composed of one immense polished diamond; high columns of stalactites, which appeared like crystal serpents twisted one with another amid garlands of flowers, sustained that brilliant ceiling. Fringes of lilies joined together, leaves of the wild vine mingled with flowers of the rosemary red as the ruby, formed festoons which were truly enchanting, and beneath a canopy formed by the crystallized waters was seen a throne of moss, soft as the skin of the ermine, yielding like the cushions upon which recline the Oriental odalisques. Softly leaning on this couch reposed the queen of this mansion of marvels; red tiny slippers covered her feet, and a gauze embroidered with gold veiled her face. When the warrior entered this retreat, she arose and drew back her veil. Her jet-black eyes were fixed on Juan de Arpide; around her coral lips hovered a charming smile, and with her exquisitely modelled hand she made a sign to the knight to come and sit by her side. Arpide obeyed, and the maidens who had conducted him disappeared.

"Juan de Arpide," she said, in a melodious voice, "you have come in here at a forbidden hour; you have surprised me in my sleep, and you interrupted my feasts; you were worthy of punishment."

"Lady!" replied Arpide, astonished at beholding such exquisite beauty, "I was unaware of your existence in these places, and if, in effect, I have committed the crimes you accuse me of, the blame is due to my evil star."

"For that reason do I forgive you," replied the charmer "Had it not been for my intervention your death would have been certain."

"How so? Do you perchance know------"

"I know all. Concealed in the shadows, I witnessed your combat of yesternight. I guessed your grounds of complaint, and when you were engaged in the duel, had you not found invisible arms in the air to ward off and lessen the blows that were directed upon you, your body would have been broken to pieces."

"And how am I to thank you, lady, for such a signal favour?" cried Arpide, fascinated by the looks and speech of Maitagarri.

"You owe me nothing. I saved your life, that is certain; and therefore that life belongs to me for the future."

"Lady!" cried the knight, looking in terror to his interlocutor.

"Do not doubt it, Juan. I think also that you ought to thank me for this new proof of my affection. I well deserve that for my love you should sacrifice that of Inez de Iturrioz!"

Juan de Arpide bent down his head and made no reply.

Maitagarri broke the silence of the knight.

"Do you not answer me? Yet so must it be. A being that, like you, penetrates into my domains never leaves it again!" And the enchantress assumed, to the astonished eyes of the warrior, the same features, the same looks, the same voice as Inez de Iturrioz.

Juan de Arpide thought he was dreaming. All the pains he had suffered in his body had left him. He no longer felt the pangs of hunger, he seemed to be drinking in life from the eyes of Maitagarri.

"Listen to me," she continued, approaching him. "I will make you the happiest of mortals. Do you desire glory? Speak, and the crown of the conqueror will ever encircle your brow. Do you wish for wealth? Ask, and you shall see palaces rising up to receive you, brilliant shields to defend you, costly robes to adorn you, maidens and pages to serve you. Do you yearn for love? You will possess mine eternally--a love which is not to be compared with any other."

"Oh, Inez, Inez!" cried the knight, half distracted.

The enchantress took his hand and imprinted a kiss on his brow. But that hand was icy cold, and her kisses had no warmth in them.

Juan experienced a feeling of terror mingled with pleasure coursing through his veins. He felt the influence of the charmed atmosphere, that it was acting upon him in a soothing manner; he felt drowsy, and a mist rose before his eyes. A heavy slumber made his eyelids droop, and he fell heavily on the bed of moss, and sleep completely overpowered him.

Then Maitagarri summoned her maidens, and they sprinkled perfumed waters on his mossy bed; they cooled the atmosphere by waving huge fans of gauze; and upon his lips they poured some drops of red liquor.

Suddenly the mysterious light which had so splendidly illumined that chamber gradually began to lose its radiance. The fairy queen gazed on the face of the sleeping knight, and a look of deep sadness overspread her countenance, as also over those of her maidens; their aerial forms became more impalpable in proportion as the light waned, and they quickly disappeared, converted into mist, which likewise dispersed, leaving the cavern in complete darkness. The clatter of armed knights was echoed among the rocks, and the songs of the linnets filled the woods. The sun was showing its rubicund face on the heights of the mountain Aya.

When Juan de Arpide awoke he found himself in the same magic chamber, his head reposing, at the feet of Maitagarri, whose velvety eyes were fixed on him as though wishful of receiving the first glance on awaking. A table covered with abundant and delicate food stood in the centre of the chamber.

VI. THE PILGRIM

Antonio wended his way to the encampment. Some of the soldiers told him that Juan de Arpide had disappeared, and that his brother Gil of Iturrioz, seeing the Franco-Navarrese army routed, and not supposing that it should ever become reorganized, had departed towards home. The other troops were also retiring.

When the youth returned home he thought that some news must have been received of the lover of his sister, and he was determined to protect her love. Great was his surprise when he only found Gil, who had brought the news that Juan de Arpide had died in battle.

The news, given unexpectedly and without any preparation, inflicted a mortal wound in the heart of Inez. A profound sadness took possession of her, and a slow, obstinate fever began to undermine her existence. Whole days would she spend seated on the trunk of the tree where she had seen her lover for the first time, and at night she used to rise stealthily from her bed to creep away and wander along the solitary fields and woods. Her brow grew pale, the light of her eyes became dimmed, her well-formed figure wasted away to a skeleton, and from a maiden of great beauty she became like a living shadow which the slightest breath of air would suffice to extinguish her life. The sage counsels of her father, the tender caresses of her mother and sister, afforded no balm to cure and comfort that sad heart, wounded to death. To the wise words of her father she would listen patiently, and reply by a sad smile; to the tender caresses of her mother by a flood of tears.

In this way passed several months. It was late in the autumn. The leaves of the trees were flying about in clouds, impelled by the north-west winds, like birds of passage when they emigrate to remote lands and climes. The blue sky was covered by the first fogs of winter, the days were visibly shortened, and the nights were lengthening over the earth. The sickness of Inez was following its course; her nightly walks had already ceased.

One night the whole family were gathered together around the hearth. The father, with his venerable head uncovered, was blessing the frugal meal which was laid on the rustic table, Gil of Iturrioz was sitting at one side of the room; Catalina was spanning flax, casting from time to time sad looks at Inez, who, propped up with pillows, her eyelids half closed, and her almost transparent hands crossed, was murmuring some words, and smiling to herself in such a melancholy manner, that her smile drew tears from those around her. Dominica was weeping, hiding her face in her hands: Antonio was convulsively clutching between his hands his wood-knife with which he was carving ingenious patterns upon a walnut-wood stick which was to serve as a staff for his dying sister. A deep silence reigned in that apartment. A storm was raging, outside when suddenly some one was heard knocking at the door.

"Go and see who is there, Antonio," said the head of the family.

"A poor stranger who has lost his way and asks for shelter," replied a voice at the door.

"God protect the traveller!" replied Pedro Iturrioz. "Come in, whoever ye may be the doors of the Basque are always open to the traveller."

The stranger entered. The young men rose up, and Antonio approached the stranger to assist him. Catalina left her wheel and placed a plate on the table. The head of the family made a sign for the stranger to sit on the settle near the fire--a seat of honour reserved for the oldest of the family, but which is always given up to the guest or the stranger.

He who had come in was dressed in the garb of a pilgrim. He appeared to be about fifty years of age; his heard was thick but snow-white; his face was dark-complexioned; his hair curly; a distraught look in his eyes; his limbs were strong and well built, although he appeared tired and weary. The coarse robe which covered him was torn and draggled, a large felt hat covered his head, and he supported himself with a long staff.

At the invitation of the host the pilgrim took the seat offered him, and partook of the supper with him.

When supper was over, Pedro Iturrioz asked the stranger to say night prayers for them, which the traveller did in a tremulous voice. Scarcely had the pilgrim concluded the prayers than a deep-drawn sigh was heard, which made them all turn round. Inez had risen up appalled; her eyes had lost their brilliancy, and were opened wide in a ghastly way; her mouth, pale and parched, articulated some sounds; while her outstretched hands and arms seemed as though they wished to draw some distant object towards them. In this posture did she remain for some minutes, to the great astonishment of all who were there. Then she slowly moved her head and fell back into her chair and into her former position.

"Inez," said Dominica, in tender accents, "do you wish for anything? '

"Nothing, my sister; I want nothing. I had a happy dream, but one which will never be realized."

The young woman once more returned to her usual listless, silent manner.

"My poor daughter!" murmured Catalina, sobbing.

"Bid me adieu, my mother!" replied Inez, looking sadly at her. "Life is fast ebbing away, and I will soon go to join my darling!"

Catalina took her daughter's hands in hers, and began to kiss them passionately.

"Is your daughter ill?" the pilgrim asked Pedro.

"The wrath of God has descended on this house," he replied. "Let us bless His holy name and submit to His loving will!"

The holy resignation of the old man visibly affected the pilgrim, for his eyes were streaming with tears.

"Can you tell me the cause of her illness?" asked the pilgrim.

"They say she is dying of love!"

"Poor child!" murmured the pilgrim.

"You say well, poor child!" replied the old man. "Before this unhappy event she was the pride of my old age and the joy of my heart!"

"Perhaps she was forsaken by her lover?"

"No; her lover was one of our neighbours, a noble, honourable man."

"And what became of him?" still asked the pilgrim.

"He died," replied the old man, bending, down his head. "He died just as we were at the point of extinguishing the feuds which had divided the two families for years, and when apprised of his noble conduct towards my daughter I

56

was ready to admit him into my house. Alas! hatred is a cursed passion; and for having harboured that passion too long in my breast God has punished me. Blessed be the justice of God, that He has thought meet to make us an example!"

"Can you tell me how he died?" insisted the pilgrim.

"He died the death I wish for my sons--on the field of battle."

The pilgrim slowly turned his head and looked towards Gil, who appeared taciturn and ill at ease, not daring to look at his sister.

"Did you say he died on the battle-field?" he asked, after some moments.

"Yes, he did," replied Pedro.

"Fighting against his enemies?"

"Yes, fighting against the enemies of his country."

Once again the pilgrim looked towards Gil de Iturrioz.

Antonio had approached his father, and was listening attentively to the dialogue between him and the stranger,

"Who told you so?" once more asked the pilgrim.

"My son, who saw him die!"

"Which of them? The youth who is listening to us, or Gil, whom I see so abstracted?"

"Gil!" replied the old man, astonished at the indiscreet curiosity of the stranger, and more greatly astonished still that he should know the name of his son.

"Gil Iturrioz in that case told you a lie!" said the pilgrim, in a ringing voice.

"Gil Iturrioz never lies!" cried the first-born of the family, leaping to his feet and threatening the stranger with clenched fist.

"Strike, knight! strike me on the face--this face so wrinkled; it will then be the second time that you do it!" said the pilgrim, bowing himself down.

The arm of the young man dropped powerless by his side in presence of that evangelical humility, and he covered his face with his hands.

"Knight!" exclaimed the pilgrim, addressing Gil, "I accuse you before your parents of the odious crime of assassination."

The bystanders shuddered on hearing these words. Inez drew herself up, and fixed all her attention on that scene.

"'Tis false, villain cried Gil, in a fury. "You may thank your luck that you are under our roof; you may thank your age that I do not pierce you through with my sword!"

"Since when do my sons forget," cried Pedro Iturrioz, with angry mien, "the duties which are imposed by the laws of hospitality? Sit down, Gil, without another word; you are accused of a crime. Señor," he added, addressing the pilgrim, "you have pronounced a grave accusation; can you prove it?"

"At this very moment, if you wish it," replied the pilgrim.

"Commence at once then," said the old man, his countenance assuming the dignity of a judge who distributes impartial justice without appeal.

"To you, Gil de Iturrioz, a Guipuzcoan knight, I address myself. Whom did you meet in the valley of Articuza about four months ago?" the pilgrim asked, in a loud tone.

Gil shuddered, and looked in terror towards the stranger.

"What was the conversation which took place between you and Juan de Arpide? Did he not offer you terms of peace?"

"Yes," replied the accused, in a low voice.

"Did he not promise you his sincere friendship?"

"Certainly."

"And instead of accepting it, did you not insult him?"

"That also is true," replied Gil, abashed.

"And to the insult did you not add the injury of striking him in the face with your gauntlet?"

The young man did not reply.

"Answer, Gil de Iturrioz," continued the pilgrim.

When you grasped the weapon was it not you the only one to attack, and your antagonist did no more than defend himself by parrying off the blows without in any way wounding you?"

Gil likewise did not reply to this question. The father was casting on his son looks of wrath; Antonio trembled with indignation; and the women appeared struck dumb with astonishment.

"To you now, old man, I address myself," continued the stranger. "Your son stumbled and fell to the ground, and when Juan de Arpide, justly irritated, might have killed him as he lay there, he nevertheless gave him his hand to assist him to rise; he then newly proposed terms of peace with him, and instead of accepting the proposals, he landed a blow at him which inflicted a deep wound in his neck, and then he cast him headlong from the summit of a rock down a deep chasm. How will you call your son in future?"

"Gil!" cried the old man, pointing to the door with an imperious gesture, "quit my house! I no longer acknowledge you to be a son of mine!"

On hearing the curse uttered by Pedro Iturrioz on his first-born, and deeply impressed by the revelation made by the pilgrim, Inez uttered a cry and fell back insensible. Catalina and Dominica remained terror-stricken.

When Gil, in obedience to his father's orders, was about to leave the paternal home, the pilgrim detained him.

"Look at your sister, who is nearly expiring; repent of what you did, and perchance there may yet be a remedy for so much evil done."

The stranger approached Inez, who was recovering from her faint--thanks to the care and attention of her mother--and, taking her hand, he said, turning towards the assembled family, "Should Juan de Arpide be still living, would you consent to his marriage with Inez?"

Antonio ran to the stranger, and quickly removed his hat; the white beard fell--for it was only a false one--and the noble countenance of the lover of Inez stood revealed before them all. A cry of surprise and joy rose from the lips of the assembled group. Inez looked at her lover; she passed her hands over her eyes, in silence moved her lips in prayer for some time, and then, throwing her arms around the neck of Juan de Arpide, poured a flood of tears of joy without saying a word.

That silence was truly sublime.

Gil turned pale with terror, because he judged that this apparition was a supernatural one. Acknowledging his evil conduct, he at length approached Juan, and in a deeply moved voice said: "My brother, plead for me before the just tribunal of my father."

*   *   *   *   *   *

At the beginning of the following month the marriage of Inez de Iturrioz with the first-born of the house of Arpide was celebrated with signal rejoicing.

EPILOGUE

Two days after the marriage of Inez and Juan, deep-drawn sighs could have been heard about midnight issuing from the valley, of Articuza. [5] Favoured by the moonlight could be seen, close to the rivulet, a decrepit old woman, pitifully torn and wounded in body. At her side were some shadows, or rather phantoms, that were beating and belabouring her unpityingly, and this punishment was presided over by the Maitagarri of the Pyrenees. Her countenance was expressive of wrath; from her eyes shot flames of fire; out of her mouth issued cries in place of words. It was no longer the beauty which had so charmed Juan de Arpide; it was a beauty of another description--that of the fallen angel when perchance it ceases for a moment to endure the torments of the lower regions.

"Cursed woman!" she said, interrogating the old woman; "of what use were your philters? Was it for this that you asked me for a sleeping child's hand? Woe to me! who placed more faith in the power of your amulets than in my own charms!"

"Pardon!" cried the witch of Zaldin, for it was none other, this poor, ill-used old woman.

"Pardon, indeed!" she replied, "when I would wish to tear your body to pieces! Die, lying one, as you have lived!" And the witch of Zaldin, unable to endure any longer this cruel and merciless treatment, fell down dead.

Maitagarri, with her phantom retinue, disappeared in the marvellous cave, out of which she did not issue again for a long time. When she once more appeared, the stronghold of Articuza had been already erected, and the noise of the colossal hammers, and the immense sheets of flames and sparks which like a volcano issued from the forge, impelled Maitagarri to forsake those parts to inhabit others more solitary--the sierras of *Ahuñemendi*.

The lifeless body of the witch turned black like coal, and a gigantic eagle took it away on the winds in its powerful clutches.

[1] Fairy, or Hade, which inhabits the lakes.

[2] Iturrioz--*Fonte fria*--the cold fountain.

[3] *The left hand of a child.* It was a general belief among the mountain dwellers of the Basque provinces that the left hand of a child, if severed during sleep, and wrapped round with curls of its own hair, became a valuable amulet which would deliver them of every kind of danger, and with it philters of different properties could also be made. There yet exists some among the rude inhabitants of the mountains of Roncal who foster this superstitious belief, although examples are unknown of this cruel mutilation ever having been effected, unless by the artifice of gipsies, *agotes*, or Jews, in very remote ages, as there still exists evidence of severe provisions having been adopted against these barbarians. It was also a popular belief that the blood of children was useful for invigorating the weak bodies of women.

[4] *Maitagarri.* Among the Basque people this stands for the "Peri," or the Genius of the Persians. According to the legend or popular tradition, this fairy, or hade, fell in love with a shepherd called Luzaide, and she took him to the summit of Ahuñemendi, where she had her palace made of crystal. This legend evidently forms the basis of the narrative which the author gives in this chapter.

[5] *Articuza.* Palace and stronghold close to the shores of that name. They are situated in the centre of the mountains of Goizueta, ten kilometres from this town, and surrounded by dense woods and forests.

Roldan's Bugle-Horn

I.

WHEN I heard this legend for the first time I was a youth. The circumstances which preceded and followed its narrative deserve to be mentioned, although they have no relation to the legend itself, but they were of such a nature that they will never be effaced from my mind, and I think will impart a greater interest to the tale.

The winter of 1829 was one of the most severe seasons known in this century. In Spain, snow fell all over the country, and even in the southern provinces, where a fall of snow, is quite a phenomenon, seen perhaps once in a century, the ground was covered by deep beds of snow, to the great amazement of their happy dwellers. But naturally where the rigour of the winter was felt more keenly was in the Basque Provinces. The roads from town to town and from valley to valley were impassable, and many houses were buried beneath the snow for days. The few travellers who were compelled to traverse the mountains encountered fearful dangers-of being lost in the drifts, or of falling into chasms, or, in truth, of being attacked by packs of famished wolves which, forsaking their usual haunts in the woods, prowled around the habitations.

On this occasion I was in Goizueta, a town of the mountains of Navarre, enjoying the delicious hams of the country which supplied the table of my uncle, the curé of that place, who was an indefatigable huntsman. The great snowstorm, which fell without intermission, did not permit us to leave the bounds of the dwelling-houses, and we eagerly awaited the weather to break up a little to enable us to go to the neighbouring mountains to hunt the deer and wild boars which abounded.

At the beginning of January the sky began to clear up, and one evening, as we were consulting together on the practicability of starting on the following morning, a stalwart Basque presented himself as the bearer of a letter from the prior of the monastery of Roncesvalles. This letter was addressed to my uncle, and in it the prior besought him in the name of their long friendship to come and pay a visit to the abbey,

ROLDAN'S BUGLE-HORN
"His shadow nevertheless wanders about these solitary plains armed to the teeth."

and bring a good pack of hounds to hunt an enormous black bear which had appeared in the neighbourhood, and which was devouring every living creature it could find.

At daydawn on the following morning we started for the abbey to the number of fourteen huntsmen and twenty dogs, the pick of the bloodhounds and mastiffs of the mountains of Navarre. At nightfall of the subsequent day we reached our destination, after traversing the. picturesque valley of Baztein, the bounds of Eugui, and the plain called the *Prado de Roldan*, the water and snow reaching in many parts nearly to our waists.

II.

On reaching the Abbey of Roncesvalles we were received by the prior and his monks, excellent men whose lives were passed in tranquil magnificence.

When I descried the lofty towers of that monastery, and beheld the strong walls which surrounded it--on seeing the houses of the inhabitants of that small town grouped around the immense extent of the monastic dwelling, it seemed to me that I was transported to other ages; and to my imagination, carried back seven centuries, the whole rose up before me as the work of a still more remote age--in one word, I found myself in the Middle Ages.

And in truth this idea was reasonable enough when I looked at our pack of hounds, on the robes in which we were dressed, on the two monks who had come forth to receive us, and on beholding the group of country people who attentively examined us, and saluted respectfully the venerable prior who was bestowing his blessing upon them with a benevolent fatherly smile, and whom the people loved as a true father. In truth, their affection for him was well merited, as they never had recourse to him in their troubles or difficulties without being relieved and comforted.

The massive doors of the monastery closed upon us, and we traversed the immense cloisters, preceded by servants bearing torches of pitched tow to light the way to the roomy, comfortable cell of the prior, where we could rest our wearied limbs and dry our soaked garments.

All this was a new scene to me, and I derived an immense pleasure in giving full play to my imagination, and allowing full scope to the ideas which continually presented themselves.

"That one is the noble lord of this fortress," I thought to myself, as I looked at the prior, who was seated close to the hearth upon which burned huge blocks of wood; "further on are his principal men; we ourselves are. the retinue of the other feudal baron, coming to form some alliance with his neighbour. I, the shield-bearer, he who removes the hood from the favourite falcon, the one who holds the bridle of the horse of the lady of the castle, he who carries the shield and the standard of its lord on the day of battle. This one--his ranger, he who arranges the hunt, who sounds the *Alhali* when the noble deer dashes out of its cover; this other------"

My soliloquy was interrupted by the ringing of the bell which announced that supper was ready. We all rose up on hearing the welcome sound, and departed to the private refectory of the prior. Another surprise awaited me in harmony with the thoughts which had been suggested to me by the scenes before me. A table of colossal dimensions groaned beneath huge haunches of venison and quarters of wild boar smoking in great dishes of pewter. Further on were dozens of trout in bright copper caseroles. Large flagons of yellow sweet Peralta, of red Tudela wine and cider, flanked this enormous supper. It was truly one of those Homeric suppers the memory of which has reached even down to our days. Yet, in spite of the abundance of food, the haunches and quarters and dozens of fish were fast disappearing, and the dishes remained empty as though by enchantment; wines and liqueurs also were consumed with incredible rapidity, and I must confess that I was one of those who most contributed to their prodigious disappearance.

During supper the whole conversation turned on the object of our journey, and the prior informed us that the bear we had come from such a distance to hunt was so formidable an animal that no one dared to venture far from the dwellings through fear of being devoured.

"We shall bring you that bear to-morrow," said my uncle, who awaited the coming hunt with all the impatience of an enthusiastic huntsman.

"Be careful what you do, my friends," replied the prior; "I am told that it is an enormous animal, very agile and exceedingly ferocious."

"Believe me, you need have no fear; and I promise you that his skin shall keep your feet warm this winter," rejoined my uncle.

"Would to God you did destroy him! for I assure you that there will be many to thank you, since the poor carriers and muleteers are quite cowed with the beast who persists in following them."

"Towards what part is the animal more frequently seen?"

"On the road which leads to the gate of France."

"What! on the path of Roldan?"

"Yes; it is about that district that he has been seen."

"'Tis well; now, gentlemen, let us retire to rest, as it will be necessary to rise early to-morrow."

The prior recited the *Benedicite*, and the servants appeared with lights, and each guest betook himself to the room assigned to him. It was eleven o'clock, for the supper had lasted long. My cousin Francisco and myself occupied a small apartment which had two long, narrow windows, from which could be descried a portion of the neighbouring forest.

I could not resist gazing on the weird scene before me: the moon was illumining with her cold white beams the landscape covered with snow, and not the smallest .cloud could be perceived on the horizon to obscure her pure light. I opened a window and stood contemplating the spectacle before me. If on reaching the monastery I had formed to myself the illusion that I was visiting one of the feudal castles of the Middle Ages, full of pages, ladies, and knights, that illusion began to assume a greater reality the moment I found myself at the Gothic window. In front of me lay a vast field mantled by hard snow, which beneath the moonbeams appeared like a spotless white carpet, the congealed icicles glistening in the moonlight as though the ground were studded with brilliants, topazes, and emeralds Further on, half hidden by a slight mist, could be seen the houses of the town of Burgete. To the right rose up the lofty peaks of the Iru and other mountains which form that severe cordillera, until they were lost in the deep blue of the atmosphere. To the left the scene was still more surprising. Immense aged oaks, pines of many years' growth, stripped of leaves, could be seen moving their snow-laden tops at the weak breath of the icy breeze. Their black trunks stood out in relief against the white background of the snowy plains, while their gigantic branches appeared like the unearthly arms of some colossal phantom.

In the midst of the sepulchral silence of night, broken only by the distant noise of the running streams, my ears perceived some unfamiliar sounds, which, though weak and far distant at first, began to swell; and that singular sound which had so struck me continued to increase--was it an illusion? Perchance it was. My heated imagination conjured up before me that heroic combat of the armies of Charlemagne against the dwellers of the mountains of Navarre. I heard the clashing of lances, the neighing of the horses, the pelting noise of stones as they struck the steel armour of the horsemen, the whizzing of the arrows as they flew across the air, the cries of the conquerors, the sighs of the wounded, the groaning of the dying; the cause of this unwonted noise was duly explained!

I was about to close the window and retire to rest when I heard truly a clear ringing cry, penetrative--a cry which was echoed by the adjoining rocks and chasms, this cry being repeated and prolonged and echoed over and over again.

"Francisco!" I cried, "tell me what this means?"

My cousin awoke up, and at that moment the weird sound was repeated.

"Oh!" replied, rising up and approaching the window, "I know what it is. It is Roldan, who is blowing his horn, asking for help."

"And who is this Roldan?" I asked.

"Do you not know? Well, he is one of the twelve, peers of France who died at the boundary," he replied, going back to bed.

I could not help bursting out laughing, but Francisco grew very wrathful at my incredulity, as he was a firm believer in ghosts, phantoms, and apparitions.

"You unbelieving Jew!" he cried, in anger; "is that all they teach you at the universities? Are there no witches? Do you not believe that the spirits appear of those who have died and were left unburied? Go to "Aquelarre" on some Saturday night, and on the next morning you will tell me what you have seen; go now, this very moment, to take a walk in that wood which lies before us, and I promise you that ere you have walked fifty paces you will meet with *Bassa Jauna*."

"Come, cousin, do not take it so to heart," I replied, as I am in total ignorance of all that passes here."

Five minutes later I was in bed and fast asleep.

III.

When the first rays of the dawn were touching the tops of the mountains which surrounded the monastery, the pack of hounds were gathered in the wide courtyard, their barking awaking the huntsmen. The yelping of the impatient dogs, the blowing of the hunting horns, the voices of those who had risen early, produced such a din, that I was forced to rise against my will and descend to join them. My uncle the cura, with his merry, happy face, breathing health, through every pore, was awaiting us surrounded by huntsmen and followed by the prior, who did not cease to enjoin us to be careful, and to take ever precaution against being suddenly assailed by the fierce beast we were going to encounter.

We joined the group, and bade the prior farewell, his parting words being, "Now, boys, keep together, and above all aim right; may you have a good day's sport; and now I shall go and celebrate mass."

Within a quarter of an hour after leaving the monastery we had lost sight of its walls, and had interned ourselves in the forest. We divided the party into couples, the better to scour the forest. We formed a wide semicircle as in guerilla warfare, and placed the dogs between the distances. In this way we proceeded to search high and low, leaving no defile unexplored, nor rock or mountain unscoured--but all in vain. The bear did not show an appearance, nor could we find the smallest trace which could afford us any clue to its haunts. In this bootless search we continued until three o'clock in the day, when it was judged prudent to return to the monastery before the night, should overtake us, wandering about those solitary places covered by snow and frost.

I was exceedingly tired from ascending and descending the rocks and mountain parts, as I was little accustomed to this kind of exercise, and my hands were raw from grasping the thorny bushes and briars when scaling the rocks and climbing up the hillsides. I threw myself down, resting against a rock; Francisco sat down by my side, and Tigre, our good dog, lay at our feet licking my hands. The other huntsmen were preparing for their return home.

"Come," I said, "let us drink a draught of wine, and then tell me something about Roldan's bugle-horn."

Ah my cousin replied, in a grave tone, "if you had passed whole weeks as I have, in the forests and woods, with no other companion but a dog and a gun, you would then know a great many things which you know nothing of. Get up and follow me, since you still wish me to tell you something concerning this French knight, and I will tell you what I have heard, but it must be related on the very spot where that brave fell and died."

I rose up, and we both proceeded to the eminence pointed out by Francisco. Nothing more grand could be imagined than the view commanded from this eminence; the virgin luxuriance of the Basque mountains, with their trees of immense height, their huge broken chasms and rocks contemporary with the creation, their tops covered with the snows of centuries, and the torrents below of turbid waters which have been flowing on from the beginning of the world. The heights on which we stood was a broken point, and on the opposite side to this division there was a huge gap, and this opening is the boundary or gate which divides it from France.

We reached the spot where Roldan died, and from whence, it is said, he still blows his horn. It is related that whenever the blast of his horn is heard the rocks fall to pieces, the mountains catch fire, and homesteads disappear by fierce storms.

"Tell me, pray tell me all about this."

"Well, then, listen."

"There was in France an emperor or king who went on from conquest to conquest, working his way towards the North. In his incursions he was accompanied by some barons of his realm, who were exceedingly brave and daring, among the number being Roldan, and he was distinguished above them all, like the tops of a beech tree rising above the other trees of the forests. Wearied of always proceeding towards the North, where he only found snow and ice, he returned to his own kingdom, and, after making some preparations, he sallied out to conquer the South. Do you see that mountain yonder, so high that its top is nearly lost in the clouds? From that mountain up to Elizondo nothing was seen but soldiers; the ground shook beneath the weight of that concourse of men covered with steel, at the head of which went Roldan. No resistance could we offer them because we were totally unprepared. They went on and reached Pamplona and conquered it; they spread themselves along the shores and they became the masters. Inebriated with such signal success, they returned to France, leaving their strongholds garrisoned. Nevertheless in that retreat there awaited them the punishment to their ambition. The whole army passed along that road covered with snow, towards where you are looking. The multitude of soldiers resembled a long serpent, whose head, led by the emperor, was concealed in Oleron, and the tail, at which stood Roldan, reached to the walls of the holy monastery of Roncesvalles. All the cliffs and chasms repeated the echoes a thousand times over, the noise of the songs, and the clamping of the horses' hoofs. Roldan had already reached to the summit of the pine plantation, which from hence looks as small as the lime tree; he was conversing cheerfully with his soldiers, when a horrible stampede was heard on the winds. They looked up in terror and saw huge masses bounding down the slopes in fearful leaps and awe-inspiring roar, and falling like hail on the troops, crushing them to the ground like so many reptiles."

"And what was that which was flying in space?" I asked, deeply interested with this picturesque narrative.

"Pieces of rock of the size of these we are sitting upon," he replied. "A fearful cry was heard in that defile. The troops mustered together, and with their shields endeavoured to offer an opposition to that shower of broken rocks, but the resistance was too weak to be able to repulse projectiles of this description. Their arms were broken, their bodies trampled, and men, guns, vehicles, and horses were crushed down, and, before many minutes had elapsed, all that road was covered over with dead bodies, broken corselets, and shields. Roldan was the only one who had been untouched by the missiles; he blew his horn asking for help, and the fierce, terrible *irrinzi*, or war-whoop, of the Basques was the response he received.

"All those mountain tops and heights were crowned, with Basques, who were hurling down broken rocks flying arrows, and even throwing huge balls of hard snow. They were commanded by Count Lobo. The count witnessed all this terrible slaughter, seated on the very spot which you are occupying. Roldan made strenuous efforts to reunite his men, and, by scaling the mountain sides, to cast the enemy from the heights. Several times did he reach as far as that break which lies two yards from your feet; but the trunk of a tree which rolled down the cliff, and other projectiles, arrested his venture.

"At length, wearied by so much wrestling, he formed a rampart with the bodies of his soldiers, and in this manner, behind this defence, he blew his horn and cursed his cousin the emperor. The sounds from his trumpet grew weaker and weaker, and as a last effort of his death agony he took his sword by the blade and cast it far from him. The sword struck this very spot, and was buried up to the hilt. The horn was silenced.

"Roldan died pierced by arrows, and surrounded by the dead bodies of his soldiers. His shadow, nevertheless, wanders about these solitary places; armed to the teeth, he is seen on the heights flinging down enormous rocks to obstruct the passage, the silent proof of his rout At times, when some catastrophe threatens the land, the sound of his horn is distinctly heard, announcing by those blasts the misfortune which is threatened. And when the anticipated calamity takes place, there are seen about these localities during the night long lines of armed men dancing to the measure of the strange music which their chieftain executes. Hapless indeed is the Basque muleteer who happens to pass at that moment."

"What happens then?" I asked.

"He will die broken to pieces against the rocks."

"So that, should these ill-omened fellows appear at this moment------"

"We should be instantly killed," replied Francisco.

"Hum, hum! I am not afraid of the dead," I replied, smiling. "I am more impressed by the presence of two living men than by all the dead bodies of Roldan and his soldiers."

"Afraid of the living?" he replied, with a contemptuous sneer. "When I have my gun loaded I fear none who may stand before me!"

I was about to reply, and perhaps start a discussion, when we heard close to us the same strange noise and ringing cry which had reached us on the previous night.

"That is your Roldan, who no doubt is coming to tear us to pieces," I said, laughing, little thinking what was the actual cause of that cry.

But I was astonished to witness the terror and ashy pallor of the countenance of my cousin, who with finger on his lips was indicating to me to keep silence. Tigre had pricked up his ears, and was uttering sinister growls.

Suddenly Francisco cried, "I have lost my bugle-horn."

"What is the matter?"

"Why, look to the right; do you not hear?"

I could certainly hear the crackling sound of dry branches as they broke under the heavy muffled tread of some one slowly advancing, but I did not apprehend what it was.

"Is it, perhaps, Roldan who is approaching?" I asked, half convinced that this supposition might be a true one.

"Who knows? Silence! quiet, Tigre!" he whispered, menacing the dog which at once lay down at my feet.

The night was fast closing in, and the mists were descending from the mountains over the valleys. All at once throughout space resounded a ringing cry far more piercing than any we had yet heard, and on turning round in the direction from whence it proceeded, we beheld in astonishment a formidable black bear about thirty paces from us, and which stood still to look at us. When I saw him, I felt the blood freezing in my veins, and almost mechanically I raised my gun to aim but Francisco cried out, as he grasped my gun, to lower it. "Do not fire, else we are lost!"

The animal was slowly advancing, growling with pleasure on seeing his coveted prey so near to him, and which he felt sure of obtaining. The beast was a huge one, and his paws, with their sharp curved claws, were truly monstrous.

"Let us prepare for a hand-to-hand fight," said Francisco, on perceiving that the animal was beginning to agitate himself. "Were I alone," he added, drawing out his long woodman's knife-------

"What would you do?" I asked

"I would lodge a shot in his body, and then pierce him through with this knife."

"Shoot him then, and if you do not succeed in killing him I will fire also."

"It is impossible," he replied, "because, should I not kill him, he would attack us and although, were I alone, I could easily defend myself, yet I could not do so with you."

"Let us run for it, then," I said.

"Run from him?" he replied, looking at me from head to foot. "You are tired out, and before we should have departed twenty paces you would feel his claws clutching at your neck. No, let us do something else."

"Let us fight him to death," I rejoined.

The bear uttered a deep growl and dashed at us. Quick as thought my cousin leaped to the front and placed his body between me and the beast. The eyes of Francisco were gleaming with a strange light, his right hand grasped the long knife, and a feverish tremor betrayed his extraordinary resolve. That wrestling would have proved an unequal one, had not another combatant appeared on the field, when the bear was at a short distance from us. The dog Tigre, which had been hitherto only yelping and watching, now leaped on to the beast with the strength and agility of dogs of his breed, and, catching him by the neck, turned him over and both rolled to the ground. The

68

rage of the bear was something terrible: he growled savagely, and set at the dog; but the latter, being agile and trained, parried the attacks of the beast with surprising skill.

"We are saved!" cried Francisco.

"Let us fire at him!" I said, preparing my gun.

"Keep quiet, for heaven's sake!" he exclaimed. Don't you see that, should we not kill him, he would turn his attacks from the dog and direct his fury towards us? Let us reserve our shot for the end."

Meantime the bear was vainly trying to catch the dog, but every time that he renewed the attack the dog would fly at him, and dig its teeth into the bear, forcing him to roar furiously.

My cousin then began to call at the top of his voice to summon the other huntsmen, if he could make himself heard by them, and they in their turn were already very anxious because we had not rejoined them. At last, after a quarter of an hour of anxious waiting, we heard the blasting of the hunting horns, the yelping of dogs, and the answering cries of our companions announcing their arrival.

When the bear heard all that noise he began to retire very slowly: we then fired two shots, and he disappeared in the wood. The huntsmen hastened up to us, nearly exhausted with fatigue, and fearful that some misfortune had happened to us.

"Pepe! Pepe! where is Pepe?" cried my uncle, in terror and out of breath.

"Here we are, uncle," I replied.

"Are you unhurt?"

"Yes, thank God; but had it not been for Francisco the bear would have torn me to pieces."

"Mercy upon us!" exclaimed all the huntsmen in one voice. "Have you seen the bear?"

"Yes, as surely as I see you!" I replied.

"Where is Francisco?" they asked.

At that moment we heard the report of a gun in the wood, followed by a fierce growl. We all ran towards the spot whence came the noise, and we found Francisco raising his gun to fire with the greatest coolness.

"I have wounded the beast," he said, as soon as he saw us coming; "if we follow the track the bear will be ours."

"But, gentlemen," said one of the huntsmen, "it is almost night."

"What does it matter?" replied Francisco, as he shouldered his gun and started in pursuit.

We all followed him, and on the snow we could plainly see the spots of blood from the wounded animal.

"He is certainly wounded," said my uncle; "therefore let us proceed cautiously. Pepe," he added, addressing me, "come close to me, do not linger behind nor separate yourself from our party."

"Come along with me!" cried Francisco, as he grasped my hand in an affectionate manner; "before the bear touches a thread of your coat he will have to tear me to pieces."

Deeply touched at this proof of his friendship I returned his grasp in silence The pack of dogs were leashed together, setting Tigre foremost, and we joined ourselves together in a close column, and, preparing our weapons, we followed for a considerable distance the track of the animal. The night quite closed in, but we were able to continue our search, thanks to, the reflection cast up from the whiteness of the untrodden snow. The footprints and occasional spots of blood from the wounded animal served as a guide, but on reaching a plain, encircled by high rocks like gradients in an amphitheatre, the trace of footprints and the drops of blood ceased. From this we inferred that the bear's den must be in some opening of the rocks standing before us, so we decided to encamp on the snow, taking all necessary precautions to spend the night in security and all possible comfort. With a quantity of dry branches we kindled a fire, fastened the dogs in couples, refreshed ourselves with food and wine, and settled to sleep. Some of the keepers took their turn to watch, and formed a sort of mounted guards. In spite of the piercing cold, somewhat modified by the heat of the fire, we soon fell fast asleep.

IV.

At daydawn we were up and commenced anew our search. We found deeply impressed footprints of the beacon the snow, and followed the track which led us to the further end of this natural amphitheatre of rocks. At the base of a high cliff we discovered an opening curtained by overhanging branches and much tangled growth, and none doubted that this opening led to the den of our enemy. We carefully examined the surroundings of this mountain, in order to discover whether there existed any other opening to this cave, but to our great satisfaction we found none. We then held a sort of council of war, to discuss the best means possible to dislodge the animal from his lair, and after some animated discussion the proposal suggested by my cousin was unanimously adopted. This was simply to place the huntsmen on the heights which surrounded the plain for safety, and the keepers with the dogs leashed together to stand at the entrance of the plain. Then to collect some branches, pile them up at the mouth of the cave and set fire to them, and by this means smoke out the beast from his lair. We accordingly perched ourselves all along the heights of the rocks, and my cousin, armed with his long knife, and followed by some of the men carrying wood, gently approached the cavern, covered up the entrance with the branches, and set fire to them. My curiosity was at its highest point, and the eyes of all were fixed on the bonfire, which was beginning to cast vivid flames and dense columns of smoke. Francisco stood on my right, and the dog Tigre on the left. Ten minutes elapsed without anything taking place, and we were beginning to think we had after all missed our mark, when we perceived the ignited branches flying in the air, and scattered about on all sides under the vigorous kicks of the bear. He appeared on the scene uttering fearful growls, and casting fiery glances around at us. When the animal found himself enclosed within that narrow circle, his fury knew no bounds. He made towards the dogs, which were all let loose together, and a terrible fight ensued. The bloodhounds covered the bear with their tawny bodies; the beast lacerating all those he could bite at with his long teeth, and in a short time out of that rolling heap of bodies came forth indescribable cries of pain, and blood flowed. Thirteen dogs fell victims, either killed or wounded, in that fight, and the rest withdrew at the call of their keepers. The bear, now fairly exhausted, sat on his haunches, unable to move, his jaws wide open, and his tongue hanging out like a sheet of red-hot iron.

"Fire altogether!" cried my uncle, and five balls entered the animal's body.

The bear gave a tremendous leap on finding himself wounded; he reared on his hind legs, gazed upon the scene around him, and with desperate bounds, horrible growls, and grinding his teeth in a fearful manner, covered with blood and froth, he dashed in the direction where Francisco and I were standing to attack us. In order to reach to where we stood, it was necessary for the animal to clamber a cliff of about sixteen feet high, upon one of the crevices of which we had taken our position. The other huntsmen did not dare to fire through fear of wounding us; nor were they able to render us any assistance, as it was too late to prevent the attack or divert the beast. Meanwhile the bear was with surprising agility clambering up, and we almost felt the hot breath of his nostrils. The huntsmen were terror-stricken: my poor uncle endeavoured to encourage us with cheering words, while a cold perspiration overspread my face. I trembled from head to foot, and I knew not what to do. I turned towards my cousin, who gave me a grasp of the hand, and, turning deadly pale, murmured, "The bugle-horn of Roldan!" The critical moment had arrived. Flight was now impossible. The bear advanced, and had already raised his huge paws to pounce upon us. Francisco leaped forward, made the sign of the cross, raised his gun, took aim, and fired. I closed my eyes. A cry of joy resounded in that enclosed plain on seeing the beast roll over, down the broken cliff, and Tigre with him. Francisco uttered an *irrinzi* of triumph, and, swiftly following the animal, he leaped down and stuck his long knife into the breast of the bear.

Three hours later, we entered the walls of the monastery bringing the dead body of the black bear, the terror of the adjacent mountains. From his body was extracted about twenty pounds of fat, and his handsome skin covered for some years the prioral couch of Roncesvalles.

* * * * * *

For a considerable time after this event I used to dream very frequently about Roldan's bugle-horn; and whenever I was troubled with these dreams I would awaken as in a fright and start up nervously, believing myself caught in the clutches of a black bear.

Jaun-Zuria, Prince of Erin

I.

A GREAT number of warriors with quivers slung on their shoulders fill the vestibule of the palace of Témora the residence of the kings of Erin, and the bards are singing to the accompaniment of their golden harps. the deeds performed in war and in the chase by the brave Morna, the sovereign of the Emerald Isles, surrounded by the blue waves. The harps of the bards are silenced; the warriors are ranged in two long files; the gates of the palace are flung open, and the aged Morna appears between his two sons, Lémor and Armin. The people flock to gaze on their king, and welcome him with acclamations of deep affection, because Morna is the *well beloved of all*, as his name signifies in the harmonious language of the verdant isles. The hair and beard of the king are white, but the snow of seventy winters has been powerless to bend the limbs of the athlete king, well developed by labour and a sober life. The loving people have also a welcome for the princes who accompany the ancient, for beautiful in body and soul are Lémor and Armin. Lémor possesses a face that is fair to behold as the snow which crowns the heights of Carmora; his hair is golden as the rays of the sun, and his eyes are blue like the flower of the flax. They depart from Témora, followed by the warriors and blessed by the women. The old men and the children gaze after their retreating forms with loving eyes and hearts until they become lost in the woods of Lena. But they are not proceeding to war--no--for see, the women do not weep on beholding their departure. The wild boar, of rough skin and long tusks, is the enemy against which they are going to wrestle in the forests of Lena. See them as they become lost in the fastnesses as soon as the dogs announce the presence of the giant of the woods. The king goes one way, and Lémor and Armin go another. The bugle of the keepers also announce the appearance of the wild boar. And the boar runs, runs, runs, destroying with his formidable tusks every dog which dares to approach him, repelling all the arrows directed against his hard rough skin. Lémor has separated himself from his brother as he had done previously from his father, and one hour had already been spent by the tired-out huntsmen in scouring the dense wood unable to vanquish the boar. The bugle announces to Lémor that the animal is running towards where he is, and the gallant huntsman prepares his bow. The tangled brushwood is seen moving at a short distance from him; the enormous head of the boar is descried, and the arrow of Lémor pierces the air. A cry of pain is heard, and Lémor hastens to despatch the animal; but the boar is not in the spot aimed at by the arrow, and the cry of pain is repeated some distance further. Lémor advances, and on separating the tangled growth of briars and brushwood behind which issued the wail, a cry of immense sorrow bursts from his breast on seeing that his father, the king of the green isles, the beloved of all, and of none more than of Lémor, is lying on the ground in a dying condition, his noble breast pierced by the dart shot from the bow of Lémor. Lémor beseeches help for his father, invoking the protection of heaven in behalf of the dying old man endeavours to return back his life--that life which is fast ebbing away--and he weeps on seeing his impotence, and his soul is filled with despair.

II.

They are returning to the palace of Témora, the princes of the Emerald Isles, and the warriors who went with them to the woods of Lena; but the bards who went out to receive them, when they perceived them returning in the far distance, do not strike their golden harps, nor do they welcome the huntsmen with songs of praise. Silent and sorrowful do the huntsmen and the bards arrive, and on learning the cause of this silence and grief the women and the old men and the children fill the air with their laments and their wails of sorrow. Morna, the beloved of all, returns, a lifeless body, conducted by his warriors, laid on a litter of funereal cypress, and Lémor and Armin appear to be dying of grief. The ancients, the chieftains of the tribes of Erin, assemble together on the following day in Témora, and after a long conference they come and stand before Lémor, the heir to the sovereignty of the Emerald Isles.

"Prince," spoke the oldest of the chiefs, "although by our laws a parricide is condemned to death, thou must not die, because, if thine arrow did wound thy father, it was not done willingly; but the crown must not be placed on the brow of one who is stained with the blood of his father and of his king, nor can he dwell amongst us. The crown of Morna must rest on the stainless brow of Armin. To-morrow at daybreak a ship will await thee in port provisioned and manned. Depart in her for ever from our isles, and may heaven protect thee wheresoever the wind and wave may take thee to!"

Lémor accedes to the decision of the chieftains of the tribes, and delivers himself up to the mercy of the winds and of the waves, with no better company than his own sorrow, his hope in heaven which knew his innocence, and two loyal servitors who had willed to share his misfortunes.

The ship, deficient of a skilful pilot, sailed on for days and nights and even months upon the boundless solitudes of the ocean, cast about like a toy at the mercy of swelling waves and the fury of the winds. Thirst at length begins to parch up Lémor and his servitors, who have no more water to drink or to cool their parched lips but the salt sea water. But just as the last ray of hope of discovering land had been extinguished, and they had abandoned all idea of meeting with the shore of any country whatever, they perceived in the far distance, amid the sea mists, a coast backed by green mountains, and they pushed on their ship towards that blessed land. That land was the one inhabited by the Cantabrians, [1] the race of giants which, five centuries earlier, Rome, the mistress of the world, had been unable to vanquish despite all her power.

The ship is closely approaching the shore. Beautiful is the land before them; more beautiful even than the isles of Erin is the continent which the prince and his loyal servitors hail with joy. The exiles leap from the ship on to the land and burst out in shouts of joy, because beneath the shade of some immense leafy chestnut trees they perceive a fountain of running water, clear as the crystalline roofs of the grottoes of Drumanar. The fresh water calms the heat which devours them. Peace comes over the soul, and sleep visits their weary eyelids. They cast themselves on a green slope covered with flowers, and soon fall asleep.

III.

Where goes the *echeco-jauna* [2] of Bustuna as he abandons the cultivation of his fields and descends to the deserted shores of Mundaca, followed by those who were assisting him at his work? Where goes the *echeco-jauna* in such haste?

From the mountain heights he has seen a little ship tossed by the waves and dashing itself against the rocks, and, as his heart is compassionate and hospitable he runs, flies to succour the wrecked ones whom he supposes must be battling with death on the shore. He stops as he descends to the plain, and those who came with him also. Three strangers are sleeping close to the fountain under the shade of the chestnut trees, and the *echeco-jauna* remains there in order to watch over and guard their steep.

The sons of the green isles awake, and they ask of the *echeco-jauna* what land that is which the winds and the waves have brought them to in their ship. And on learning that it is the land of the invincible Cantabrians, they raise their lips to heaven and thank God for having conducted them to the country of the first heroes of the universe. Under the roof of Bustuna they find an hospitable asylum, those exiles from Erin; but very quickly does it become known throughout the *Euskarian* mountains that among them dwells a son of kings, and the aged Lekobide, the chieftain of the *Eskaldu-nac*, [3] and descendant of the glorious leader of the same name who humbled the pride of the Cæsars, and whom the Basque people sing praises in their songs, sends messengers to the Prince of Erin to offer him a home in the valley of Padura. Lémor contemplates with delight the supreme happiness of the land on reaching the dwelling of the Basque chieftain. An aureole of glory encircles the venerable brow of Lekobide, and another of beauty and chastity that of the youthful Luz, the daughter of the chieftain of the Eskaldunac.

Months have passed since Lémor came to dwell in the home of Lekobide, and for months has he been striving to quit the valley of Padura, because as a good knight and a good Christian he is ashamed to live in idleness meanwhile that the sons of Agar are trampling on the holy cross beyond the Ebro. For months has he wished to offer his arm to Fernan Gonzalez, the Count de Castile, but he is always held back by the pleadings of Luz and Lekobide; and, more than all, is he detained by a mysterious power which dwells in his heart. Warlike exercises and the chase restrains his steps. When departing from Padura he wends his steps towards the lofty mountains that command the view of the valley to pursue the wild boar and the deer, Luz goes to the window with saddened looks to watch the stranger from the valley, and the stranger turns back seeking Luz at the window.

IV.

The Eskaldunac are free, free as the breeze and the birds of their mountains. They have no lord to whom they owe vassalage, nor do they possess other laws than those written in the consciences of their chiefs, who judge the culprit and adjust contentions under the shadow of the holy tree of Guernica. Beyond the hierarchy of virtue and of intelligence and of age, there is but one hierarchy in the land of the Eskaldunac. The Eskaldunac elect a chief who is ever ready to lead them to the combat whenever the stranger invades their free land; and this glorious title they bestowed on Lekobide more than half a century before in consideration of his virtue, his intelligence, his valour, and his glorious name.

One day, when the Euskaro patricians were assembled together under the holy oak of Guernica, one of them remarked that Lekobide was aged and impotent, and therefore incapable to take the command of the armies of the Eskaldunac on the day when the stranger should invade the land. Then a patrician of a century old spoke in the name of the assembly:

"Fifteen years have passed since Leyalá, the most valiant and loyal dog of our mountains, watched day and night at the door of his master. "Leyalá is old," said one day the *echeco-jauna*, and on that night a new guardian was installed in the post in which Leyalá had grown old.

"The fox which had been scared away from afar by Leyalá fifteen years ago, and which he had scented from a great distance, came that very night, unfelt by the young dog, and ate up the fowls of the *echeco-jauna*. And Leyalá, who, sad and broken in heart, had left the fern-bed in which he had slept for fifteen years at the door of the homestead, in order that a stranger should occupy his post, was found dead on the following morning, although the *echeco-jauna* had prepared a bed for him softer and more sheltered than the one in which he had lain for fifteen years."

Thus spoke the patrician of a century old, and since then no one ever remarked that Lekobide was aged. Neither Lekobide himself remembered his age, because the youthfulness of his spirit does not permit him to think on the age of his strong arm.

But hark! a low rumour is heard, and an unusual agitation unknown for years spreads across the valleys and along the range of the Basque mountains, and numerous scouts, their hearts full of indignation, hasten to the door of Lekobide, calling out--

"*Quidaria*! [4] a formidable army appears on the cordillera of Orduña, and alas! for the *Eskaldunac*, should the *irrinzi* [5] not be quickly heard on our mountains.

Lekobide rises up brimming over with wrath. "Blow the five bugle-horns on the five Basque mountains; for none must reach the Tree Malato of those who would dare in warfare to trample down our free dwellings! Give me my coat of mail, and the lance which seventy years ago accompanied me to the combat!" And Lekobide quickly puts on the coat of mail, and his body bends beneath the weight of his armour. Lekobide grasps the lance, but his arm is powerless to hold it. Then does the glorious chieftain remember his age and trembles; and, humbled and despairing, he falls down at the threshold of the door.

Meanwhile the alarm flies along the Basque mountains and valleys, and in answer to the call to war many Basque warriors are coming down to the valley of Padura, imploring their revered chieftain to lead them to battle. A ray of hope suddenly illumines the venerable countenance of Lekobide which had been so full of despair.

"Prince of Erin cried the old man, addressing the son of Morna, "take my coat of mail and my lance, and fill my place of command at the head of the Euskaro legions!"

"Señor!" replies Lémor, "I will fight against the enemies of thy land in which I have received such generous hospitality, but it will be in the soldier's ranks. Seek a chieftain more worthy than I to lead thy warriors to the combat."

All the Euscarian warriors who had descended from the mountains to the valley of Padura joined their pleadings to those of Lekobide, but the modest Prince of Erin insists on marching to war only on condition of fighting. in the ranks with the humblest wrestler.

"As long as thou livest, thou wilt be the leader and champion of the Eskaldunac, because I am powerless to be so," said Lekobide, with universal assent; but Lémor still continues to refuse to accept the glorious title offered to him.

"Thou art the son of kings, and art worthy to command vassals," exclaim the ancients of the twenty valleys gathered together in the valley of Padura; "the free land of the Euskaro confers upon thee the sovereignty if thou dost consent to take the command of our armies."

The prince of the green isles refuses the sovereignty of the Eskaldunac. And while all this contention takes place, more scouts appear on the field to announce that the army of the enemy has passed the Tree Malato, and are descending the mountain slopes, like a raging sea, carrying all that opposes its progress.

"Oh, Prince of Erin!" cries Lekobide, "if in my veins flowed the blood of kings I would then tell thee--Lead the Eskaldunac legions on to battle, cast out of our free land the stranger, and on returning from the combat thou wilt sit at my hearth, and I will bestow on thee the title of son!"

Lémor directed a glance full of love and hope towards Luz; and, as though he had read on the brow of the maiden the reply his soul yearned to hear, he cried out, as he donned the coat of mail and grasped the lance of Lekobide:

"Old man! may God permit me to be seated at thy hearth and hear from thy lips the name of son!"

V.

Upon the five highest mountains of the free land is heard the blast of the trumpets, and that warlike sound is answered throughout the valleys and mountains by the powerful *irrinzi*. Every man with sufficient strength to cast an arrow, wield the sword, the lance, or battleaxe, speedily rises up, quits his house, and proceeds toward the valley of Padura, whose plains and heights can scarcely hold the thousands of Basques that are collecting together in answer to the call of their Country. This call or summons is not issued without good cause, for the enemies are many, and they are already approaching the valley of Padura as though to challenge the chieftain, who they are well aware dwells there.

The armies which invade the Basque mountains are not composed of those brave legions of Castile and Leon, who so often planted the cross of Christ over the tents of the Mussulman; nor are they led by the kings of Leon or the Counts of Castile. These legions are composed of low adventurers, who defame the Christian name from the banks of the Ebro to the shores of the Tagus, and are commanded by *Ordoño the Wicked*, the vile usurper of the crown of *Sancho el Craso*, and who, cast forth from his Leonese throne, wishes to drown his disappointment in the noble blood of the Eskaldunac, and raise up on the Basque mountains a new throne upon which to sit.

The Basque army, led by Jaun-Zuria, as the people style the Prince of Erin, goes out to encounter the stranger, who is already appearing on the mountain heights that overlook the valley of Padura, and Sancho de Esteguiz, the lord of the Duranguesado, leaves his palace of Tarisa to lead the Duranguese, who are longing to fight by the side of their brother tribes, commanded by the prince. The combat is a fierce one, and its frightful din thunders throughout the hitherto peaceful mountains of the Euskaros. A dense cloud of arrows obscures the sunlight, enormous boulders of rocks wrenched by the herculean arms of the Eskaldunac are cast upon the armies of Ordoño, dismembering and crushing and terrifying them. The axe and the lance, the swords of the Basque warriors are fast cutting down the invading legions on the broken rocks of Padura. But the desperation of Ordoño incites him to make a supreme effort to reanimate the courage of the adventurers, and the victory is still undecided.

"Death to the leader of the Eskaldunac!" cries Ordoño, "and then the victory will be ours!" And he runs to encounter Jaun-Zuria, who at the same time fights, and commands his army in the thickest of the fray.

The son of the kings of Erin goes out in his turn to meet the ambitious chief of the invaders, and closes with him in a fierce match. The lance of Lekobide, wielded with Titanic force by the Prince of Erin, pierces through the breast of Ordoño, who expires uttering a roar of desperation which resounds throughout the mountains of Padura like that of a wounded lion. But alas! a stone flung by the enemy wounds the noble forehead of the lord of the Duranguesado, for whose life the Prince of Erin would willingly have given his own!

Disorder reigns now in the disbanded legions of the stranger, and they flee in terror back from whence they came, marking their footprints with blood and fire. The Eskaldunac follow them to the cordillera of Ordoño, and there, wearied with so much slaughter, and beholding their country once more happy and free, they return to rest and to celebrate their glorious triumph beneath the shades of the Tree Malato.

VI.

Nearly ten centuries have passed since the Eskaldunac, led by the exile of Erin, sent a thrill of joy and triumph among the people on the fields of Padura. Should you desire to visit these fields, do not seek on the map for the name of Padura, because they have changed this name for that of Arrigorriaga, which in the rich and venerable language of the Euskaro is equivalent to *reddened stones*. The rocks which bristle on the tops of the mountains of the ancient Padura presented for a long time the colour of the blood which the hordes of *Ordoño the Wicked* poured upon them, and for this reason was the ancient name of Padura altered to that of Arrigorriaga.

Proceed to the parochial church of the valley of Arrigorriaga, and there, close to the font of holy water, you will see a sepulchre. Ask the simple villager who it is that reposes in that sepulchre, and he will tell you that there lies a prince called Ordoño, who strove to rob the Basque people of their liberties, and was killed by Jaun-Zuria, the first Lord of Biscay. After this, examine the dusty archives of the temple, and if you understand the changeless and eternal language of the Eskaldunac, you may read in some worm-eaten parchments, yellowed by age, that in this temple were joined together the daughter of Lekobide with the son of a King of Erin.

[1] *Cantabrians*. A people of Hispana Tarraconeza, between the Pyrenees and the ocean, inhabiting Navarre, Biscay, Alava, and Guipuzcoa.
[2] *Echeco-jauna*. The master of the house, or proprietor.
[3] *Eskaldunac*. Some write it *Escualdunac* (from *escua*, hand, *alde*, right, *dunac*, those who have), a name which the Biscayans, or Basque people, give to themselves. In their dialect they call themselves *Euskarians*. This dialect, the wise Humboldt considered, was the most remarkable language of all he was acquainted with.
[4] *Quidaria*. Chieftain.
[5] Irrinzi. The shout or call of war.

The Branch of White Lilies

A TRADITION.

I.

IN the narrow deep valley along which runs the turbulent stream of Cadagüa [1] to empty itself into the sea which extends its arms as though to receive it, there is a high, noble bridge. The bridge of Castrejana, for such is it called, was constructed by Mestre Pedro Ortiz de Lequetio, and was commenced on the 9th of June, 1435, and concluded on the 4th of May, 1436. We learn this important fact from some curious historical notes which were found about the year 1730 among the papers of an Augustinian monk of Bilbao; nevertheless the people maintain that the said Mestre did no more than appropriate to himself a work which had cost the evil one many labours, as it was this dire enemy (that never beholds the countenance of God) who was the real constructor of the bridge of Castrejana.

We shall relate this curious story just as it was told to us by the dwellers of Irauregui and Zubileta, who affirm that ever since Mestre Pedro Ortiz de Lequetio usurped from the devil the glory of having constructed the bridge of Castrejana, the evil one had been so furious with the plagiarists that, whenever he can catch them in a lonely spot, he subjects them to great barbarities.

About the year 1485 there existed on the right margin of Cadagüa a humble dwelling-house, surrounded by a splendid market-garden, and protected by a circle of fine fruit-trees; while behind the house there was an apple orchard, which stretched along the base of Pagazarri. In the house of Castrejana, for such was the dwelling called, there resided a poor widow, and her daughter Catharina, who was about eighteen years of age. Catharina was the pride and charm of the valley, and from Burceña down to Alonsótegui there was no one but loved her for her goodness and admired her for her beauty. Her mother was advanced in years, and little able to attend to household duties; but the industrious daughter perfectly supplied the deficiency of hands in cultivating the market-garden, the care of the orchard, and tending to the herds. Moreover she conducted the sales, in the markets of Bilbao, of the fruit, milk, and vegetables, which formed the principal resources for the support. of the humble dwellers of Castrejana. Catharina was always at work and always cheerful. She would go singing to draw water from the fountain close to the chestnut wood on the river side, and with a song on her lips she would return. To the market of Bilbao she proceeded, singing all the way, and also returned singing until she passed the chestnut plantation of Altamira, when she always hushed her song for a few moments. Singing she worked in the garden, and gathered the fruit from the trees, or led the cattle to drink on the banks of Pagazarri.

On the other side of the river stood the house of Iturrioz, whose lands extended to close upon the fountain of the chestnut wood, from which no doubt it derived the name of *Fonte fria*--the cold fountain. Whenever Catharina went to the fountain to draw water, the lads of Iturrioz, who worked on his estate, used to start a lively chat with her, and Martino, the oldest of the lads, hastened down to the valley to offer her the best fruit of the trees on the estate.

Martino and Catharina had loved one another almost from childhood, and their parents had arranged a marriage between them which would be celebrated when the sowing of the maize, which takes place in May, should be ended, as Martino wished to help his father and brothers before leaving them to reside on the lands of Castrejana.

II.

On a dark stormy night a man knocked at the door of the widow's house, and Catharina, taking a candle, opened the wicket window of the door and asked the stranger what he wanted.

"I have come from Bilbao, and am going towards Galdemes," replied the traveller, who by the candlelight appeared to be a youth dressed in a black suit. "The river is no doubt swollen, and the night is too stormy to be able to cross in safety the high rocky mountains through which I have to journey. Give me shelter for this night, and by daybreak I shall proceed on my journey safely."

Catharina consulted with her mother, and, with her advice, she opened the door to admit the stranger. He was a young man with a handsome face and a very sweet voice, yet there was something in his voice and in his countenance which destroyed all the charm; and his bright eyes, his constant smile, and his measured, low tones and melodious accentuation rather annoyed than pleased. While the widow conversed with the traveller, the daughter was busy preparing the supper.

When the stranger finished his supper, the old woman said to him, "We have not yet said our night prayers, and if you are willing we shall be happy if you join us."

The youth made a sign of displeasure, and replied that he was very tired, and as he had to be up very early he would prefer to retire.

The widow lit a candle and led the way to a chamber, where they hastily made up a bed for him, and arranged the room as well as they could in their humble way. The window of this chamber was open, and through it came the perfume of the flowers in the garden after the rain, and more particularly was the scent perceived, above all the other flowers, of a fine plant of white lilies which grew just beneath the window, and the long stem of blossom almost reached the window-sill.

"What a rich perfume that white lily is shedding!" said the mother of Catharina, as she approached the window.

"What lily is it?" asked the traveller, with a sneer on his lips.

"One which my Catharina cultivates every spring to place on the lady altar of Begoña." [2]

The stranger made a rude gesture, and the old woman, perceiving that he was in no humour for talking, bade him good-night and retired.

The chamber occupied by mother and daughter had a window which also looked out on the garden, and was on the same side of the house as the room occupied by the stranger. Before closing the window Catharina put out her head to breathe the night breeze laden with the scent of flowers, and great was her dismay and surprise to see that the stranger was drawing out his right hand in which he held a hook with which he was endeavouring to reach the lily, no doubt to break the stem.

"Oh! what is he going to do?" asked Catharina, in alarm. "That man must be the evil one!"

The hand armed with the hook instantly was withdrawn. The mother then related to her daughter how displeased the stranger had manifested himself when he knew that the lily was destined to deck the Virgin's altar; and Catharina, fearing lest she should find her beautiful lily destroyed, which she had tended and watched over with such loving care, were she to leave it on the plant until the morning, quietly went down to the garden and cut the lily stem from the plant and brought it up to her room with the greatest care lest it. should become broken.

III.

The rain, which had partly subsided during the night, quite ceased at daybreak, and the traveller rose early, saying that he must try and cross the river before the currents should swell it, and he be unable to cross over. Catharina had a great wish to ask him why he had attempted to destroy her beautiful lily, but she did not dare to do so, as there was something in the face and looks and voice of the stranger which instilled fear and terror--she knew not why. Catharina and her mother besought him to stay a few moments until they prepared breakfast for him, but he insisted on departing at once and asked what he was indebted to them for the supper and accommodation.

"You owe us nothing but a good will," both the women replied.

"Very well, I am much obliged to you, and wish you very good health," said the stranger, and he departed, fording the Cadagüa along some enormous stones laid across, which then stood in the place of a bridge, and on the very spot where at the present day stands the bridge of Castrejana.

The fears of the stranger were well founded that he might find the river quickly impassable, for when he forded it the water was already beginning to cover the huge stones.

Catharina looked out from the side of the house which faced the river, and divided her attention between the traveller, who was hastening to take the road to Iturrioz, and Martino, who was mending a broken paling at the further end of the garden, and through which some goats had made their way into the field. This paling was on the side of the high road along which the stranger had to pass. This unknown visitor stopped to speak to Martino as he passed him. The distance and the noise of the river rushing down prevented Catharina from hearing what they said, but she noticed that Martino grew wrathful, and looked towards the house of Castrejana with menacing gestures. We know not whether it was from want of water in the house, or to have a chat with Martino, that Catharina lifted a pitcher to her head, and, telling her mother that she was going for water before the river should become so swollen that it would be impossible to cross it, she started off; but on reaching to the bank she had to turn back, as the water completely hid the stones, and the current was fearfully rapid.

A little later, Catharina, with a basket of vegetables on her head and the branch of white lilies in her hand started from home, taking the road to Bilbao, as she did every morning, to sell her goods in the market; but this morning she did not trip along with a light heart, nor did she sing as usual, but went her way silently and sad. In going and returning from Bilbao, on passing Altamira, she always stopped singing and knelt at the foot of the giant chestnut tree from whence could be descried the church of Begoña. On that morning she knelt as usual, and prayed more fervently than ever, and she even wept while she prayed. What change was this that had been worked in poor Catharina? She could not tell; but she felt in her heart a deep sadness as though some great misfortune was threatening her.

She reached the market-place of Bilbao, and while she sold her vegetables she watched her lily so that no one should break her branch. Many persons, charmed by the lovely flowers, wanted to purchase them, but Catharina would reply that she could not part with her flowers at any price, because she had brought them with her, not for sale, but to take them to the church of Begoña and deck the Virgin's altar with them as her offering.

When she had finished her sale, she went to the church, placed her beautiful lilies on the altar of Our Lady, and crossing again the Ibaizabal by the only bridge which then existed--which is the one called now the bridge of Saint Anthony--she went towards Castrejana. The river Cadagüa continued rising, because during the morning it had rained in torrents all over the Encartaciones.

Catharina kept looking towards the fields and house of Iturrioz, but did not see Martino. What was her surprise and terror, when the sun was sinking behind the mountains, to perceive the youth ascending the slope towards Baracaldo, above Zubileta, which is on the opposite bank of the Cadagüa, and that he was furnished with weapons, and clad in a coat of mail such as was worn by warriors in that epoch by various bands.

The bands called Onhacino and Gamboino were not then devastating the seigniority of Biscay and the Encartaciones, but were contending with out ceasing against the districts of Castile, particularly on all the land along the Ebro from Puentelarra to Valdivielso, commanded by the Salazares and Velascos, and they had constantly in Biscay agents who were charged to enlist men, who, allured with flattering promises of much glory and renown, had found to their cost nothing certain but a probable grave amid the rocks.

Catharina ran to the river shore and waited for Martino to reach the opposite margin; and in truth Martino did arrive, but it was to fling a folded parchment fastened to a stone across the water to Catharina, and continued to walk towards the house of Iturrioz, while Catharina in dismay read the following lines which had been written by Martino upon the folded parchment:

"I would sooner die far from hence, fighting against the enemies of the Salazares, than die here combating against your faithlessness and want of love. At midnight I join other young men beneath the chestnut tree of Iturrioz, and with them shall depart to the suburbs of Castile, where I hope death or absence will make me forget you."

IV.

The bells of the monks of Burceña were ringing for prayers, and Catharina was weeping bitterly in despair on seeing that the time was fast speeding away, and the hour approached in which Martino was to depart, perhaps never to return, and never more to see him. In vain did she look at the flowing water, waiting to discover the stones which served as a bridge; the stones remained concealed beneath the swollen currents which every moment swept down with greater power and roared with greater fury.

"What have I done, Holy Virgin," she would cry out in her deep sorrow, "that Martino should thus doubt me, and be going away to die in the wars which are destroying the bravest knights and the most honoured youths of Biscay? Some dreadful misunderstanding or some calumny has no doubt taken place which has made us both wretched. A single word from me would at once undeceive Martino and dissuade him from his sad resolve, yet I cannot approach him, nor

even speak to him, because the river, wild and swollen, interposes between us. Ah! I would give my life to be able to cross this furious current before the bells of Burceña chime the hour of midnight, and each stroke of the hour tells me that no longer will there be any happiness, either for Martino or myself, in this world!"

Thus spoke the hapless Catharina, as she wept at the foot of the chestnut tree, and looked towards the river in hopes of its subsiding, and of discovering the stones, over which she had so often merrily passed, and which now were under water, and then turning towards the house and fields of Iturrioz sought the well-known form of Martino, who, alas! did not appear as was his wont to do, frequenting the river shore to exchange a loving word with his beloved Catharina.

Suddenly she heard footsteps behind, and on turning round she saw coming up to her the mysterious visitor of the previous night, he who had sought a shelter at her mother's house. A hope, wild, because it was founded on an absurdity, beamed over the soul of Catharina.

"From this," she said to herself, "up to Aranguren, which is on the boundary of the valley of Salcedo, there is no bridge whatever, yet this man has crossed the river at no great distance from here. Perhaps some of the gigantic trees growing on the shores have been wrenched by the storm and fallen down across the stream, and, enabled the man to cross over as though it were a bridge. Should it be so, this man can tell me, and then I shall be able to cross over and see Martino in time to prevent him from going to the wars."

All this did Catharina turn over in her mind during the brief moments of surprise occasioned by the appearance of the man.

"By what part of the river did you cross?" she anxiously asked of the stranger.

"I crossed over by the bridge of Aranguren," he replied,

"How could that be, for the bridge of Aranguren stands some three leagues from here?"

"By making prodigious efforts!" he cried.

"Prodigies indeed! Ah, would that I could work them as you have done!"

"Which would you wish to do first?"

"I would wish to cross the river."

"In that case it would be necessary to have a bridge to be able to cross the river."

"Most certainly."

"I can make one."

"How? perhaps by felling some of the trees and placing them across on both sides of the river?"

"That would be impossible: because the river is very wide, and none of the trees, however high, would reach across to the opposite shore."

"How then?"

"By constructing a stone bridge."

"That would take too long a time, for I must cross over, at latest, when the bells of Burceña strike the hour of midnight."

"I can easily erect it by that hour."

"Do it then."

What will you give me if I do?"

"My life."

"Your life is not enough payment for me."

"What more do you require?

"I must have your soul!"

"Well, then, have it, so that you erect the bridge without delay."

Catharina seemed to be under some irresponsible influence when she uttered these words, and knew not what she said. But scarcely had she spoken these wild words than reason asserted itself in her mind, and she clearly comprehended the grave import of her words, and she then wished to recall them, or at least to explain them; but the mysterious stranger had already departed far from that spot; while on the river shores, obscured by the shades of night, which was a very dark one, nothing was heard but the noise of hatchets, pickaxes, spades, saws, and hammers, as though a multitude of workmen, stonemasons, carpenters, and other artificers, were digging, sawing wood, cutting huge blocks of granite and stone, and laying the foundation, erecting the pillars, and forming the arch of the bridge.

The idea that this man dressed in black was the evil one began to take possession of the imagination of Catharina, and what more terrified her than the thought of losing her lover was the conviction that she was going to lose her soul. Catharina in her distress cried out to that man, "Do not erect that bridge at the expense of my soul, because I do not wish to give it to you!" But her voice was drowned in the noise of the rushing waters of the Cadagüa, and the uproar of hammers and pickaxes which continued to be heard on the river banks, as though an invisible legion of carpenters and stonemasons were working there; while amid that unearthly roar the hapless girl seemed to hear a voice rising above it all which replied to her, "It is too late! It is too late!"

The night advanced, and Catharina amid the gloom saw rising on either side of the river white columns, which were no doubt the base or buttress to sustain the arch of the bridge. A gleam of hope suddenly strengthened the fainting heart of Catharina, and she at once started towards the coast of Castrejana, and on reaching to the foot of the chestnut tree of Altamira, she fell on her knees, and, looking in the direction of the temple of Begoña, she invoked the protection of the Virgin, saying, "Holy Mother of God! save my soul which is in peril of losing its eternal salvation

The valley of Ibaizabal was as darksome as the depths of Cadagüa; but scarcely had Catharina said these words of fervent prayer, than it appeared to her that a soft resplendency illumined the valley, which for a thousand years has been protected and watched over by the Mother of God from the heights of the hills of Artagan. What light could it have been? Ah! perchance it was that of hope! Enlightened and strengthened by this light, Catharina descended the slope of Castrejana. The soft light which shone over the valley of the Ibaizabal [3] was spreading also along the valley of the Cadagüa, and by its gleams Catharina saw that the two buttresses which she had seen, or imagined she saw, rising up on both shores of the river, and the erection proceeding on either side, were meeting in the centre to form a perfect arch. Towards the side of Iturrioz there shone a light similar to a flaming torch, which began to descend to the chestnut wood and disappeared among the leafy branches. The heart of Catharina beat fast in anguish. That light appeared to her to indicate that midnight was fast approaching, and Martino must be quitting the paternal home, and was about to forsake, perhaps for ever, his native valley.

Catharina looked steadfastly before her, never removing her eyes from the bridge, which now was almost finished, and nothing was wanting for its completion but the key-stone. Suddenly a form was seen ascending the almost finished bridge. It was the form of a beauteous lady, who carried in her hand a branch of lovely white lilies, and as she reached to the open gap between the two sides of the arch she laid the stem across the opening and disappeared, leaving a luminous trail, which extended to a great distance, until it eventually became lost in the depths of the valley of Ibaizabal.

When Catharina turned her gaze away from the east, where that singular vision had disappeared, and looked towards the bridge which was constructed in such a, marvellous manner, she saw the man in the black suit holding in his hands an enormous block of stone, which he carried as easily as though it were a light ball, and running up along the arch was about to place the heavy slab in the opening and thus complete the bridge. However, in spite of all the efforts of the artificer to fix the slab or block in the opening, the slab did not fit in. The man hammered desperately at the stone, accompanying, each blow with an oath, but the stone resisted all his efforts, as though it were prevented fitting in by a strong bar of iron laid beneath. And the man in black redoubled his furious efforts as he heard the sound of the bells of the monastery of Burceña vibrating through the valley announcing the midnight hour, and on hearing the chimes he uttered a cry of desperation, and cast himself headlong into the river, and was carried away in the furious currents and disappeared altogether. At the moment when he flung himself into the seething waters a sound was heard on the bridge like the noise of a branch snapping in two, and in that instant the key-stone, or huge slab which the man in black had been unable to fit in, fell gently into its place, and the bridge remained perfect; while a huge cataract of water now descended roaring along the windings of Alonsótegui, carrying down towards the Zubileta all the scaffolding and temporary erections employed in building the bridge. Catharina then rapidly crossed over by the bridge which had been so marvellously constructed, and ran to the chestnut wood of Iturrioz.

Half an hour later a number of youths, clad in mail and armed with war weapons, ascended along the Cadagüa, lamenting that Martino de Iturrioz should prefer the effeminate blandishments of love to the manly and glorious exercise of war.

Martino, leading Catharina by the hand, accompanied her to the house of Castrejana, where he bade her an affectionate farewell, passed over the Devil's Bridge, sped across the lands, and returned to the house of Iturrioz.

Between the joints of the enormous blocks of stone which constitutes the key-stone and the lateral slabs of the bridge, there used to spring up every year some beautiful white lilies, which the damsels of the valley of Ibaizabal gathered on the morning of St. John's Day, and these flowers were called *Cataloros*, a name derived from the Basque word *Catalenlorac*, which means "flowers of Catharina," but owing to the great fall of rain and inundation which occurred on the 22nd of September, 1523, the foundations of the bridge were shaken and the buttresses unsafe, and it was found necessary to substitute smaller stones to replace the massive key-stone, which it was feared would fall down and destroy one of the noblest and most elegant bridges of the Basque provinces.

[1] See *Cadagüa*, in Glossary. [2] *Begoña.* See Glossary. [3] *baizabal.* See Glossary.

The Song of Lamia

[1]

I.

IT was the first third of the seventeenth century. In those days the slopes of the mountains which encircled the valleys were densely covered with luxuriant trees; these plantations began to disappear during the civil wars, and in a greater degree after the war, on account of the increase of naval construction in the building trade of Zurrosa, Duesto, Salve, and Ripa.

When beautiful chestnut woods and forests of oak covered the southerly brows of Archanda and Berriz, which now are almost bereft of vegetation, and also along the base of the valley where, God be praised! they substituted for the ancient trees the no less beautiful embellishment, and one more useful, of numbers of *quintas*, splendid houses, gardens, orchards, and manufactories, there lived a happy couple.

On the brow of the mountain Berriz, in the centre of a plantation of luxuriant chestnuts, there existed, during the three first decades of the seventeenth century, a house surrounded by some acres of arable land. That homestead, and the happiness of its inmates, no doubt inspired in the people a song or ditty which I heard for the first time in those plantations, and which runs as follows:

> Tener herencia en campo bello,
> Yuna casa en la herencia,
> Yen la casa pan y amor,
> Es grande felicidad.

("To possess an inheritance in a lovely land, and in that inheritance a house, and in that house bread and love, is indeed a great happiness.")

And in truth they were very happy, Martin and Prudencia, as they were called by the dwellers of Aurrecoechea. Their love began in the holy occupation of labour.

Prudencia dwelt in the house of Aurrecoechea, whose acres had to yield the sustenance necessary for herself and her mother, the only member remaining of her family, and she was too old and helpless to work. In another house, close to that of Prudencia, lived Martin, who also had to support by his labour in the paternal home his aged parents who could no longer earn their bread.

Some of the work done by the tillers of land in the Biscayan provinces demands the united labour of two or more persons. Hence it is that a woman is never seen alone digging or tilling the ground, because the field labourer or farmer, who has no one of his family to assist him in his hard work, and is too poor to hire labourers and pay wages, digs in exchange with any of his neighbours who may be similarly situated; that is to say, they join together and work alternately on each other's land.

When the season for digging commences, which is that when the sky begins to clear up and shows a cloudless blue, the birds to sing on the trees, and the flowers to spring up on the banks, Martin and Prudencia used to join together and work alternately on each other's land; and in that occupation, which I do not hesitate in calling a holy one, since it is a holy labour, that of him who sows the land by the sweat of his brow in order that it may produce the fruits with which to maintain his family--there sprang up in the hearts of these two, honoured and comely beings a pure affection which grew and became strengthened.

It is easier to comprehend than it is to explain the sweet charm which their labour must have possessed for those two young people, that labour shared together, and in which they learned to love one another in a supreme degree. Both lost almost at the same time their parents, and both felt that they remained alone in the world; but when Prudencia saw Martin in his house, and Martin in that of Prudencia, a hope rose up which smiled upon their lives, and then both felt that they were not left alone in the world.

One lovely spring morning Prudencia left her house at the same moment as Martin left his, and both met on the slope of the hill and descended to the plain, where they entered the Church of San Pedro de Deustua. An hour later they ascended the mountain, Prudencia leaning lovingly on his arm, and instead of parting company to enter each one into their house, they both went into the house of Prudencia, because it had become a fact that love and the permission of the church had rendered common property both their inheritances.

For two years did Martin and Prudencia live together. Poor indeed they were as regards the riches of this world, but rich in love and happiness, and no doubt it was then that some versifier of the mountains of Goyerry or of the plains of Olaveaga composed the Basque ditty which I have humbly rendered into English. But as in this world there is never complete felicity, so also was the happiness of Martin and Prudencia incomplete, because often when Martin heard in Aurrecoechea the bells of Santa Maria de Begoña ringing for mass, he used to say-- "We must have a mass said to beseech the Virgin to implore our Lord to give us, through her intercession, what is wanting to complete the joy of our home."

"Yes, we must indeed," Prudencia would reply, blushing and full of joy.

II.

Martin and Prudencia were overjoyed when the young wife felt that their desires were to be realized, but their joy was very quickly turned into sorrow.

On one autumn evening they were both in the chestnut wood. Martin had climbed a tall tree the branches of which he was beating with a long stick, while Prudencia gathered the chestnuts, as they fell, into a basket. Suddenly a cry was heard in the chestnut plantation where Martin was, and he fell to the ground uttering a cry of terror, followed by another from Prudencia. She ran to help her husband, and filled the wood with cries for assistance; and the neighbours quickly hastened to render help; but it was all of no avail. Martin, who had fallen to the ground owing to the breaking down of the branch upon which he was standing, had ceased to exist. In the bitterness of her grief Prudencia heard the bells of Begoña, which happened to be tolling for the dead; and she prayed in her agony that the Lord might relieve her of the weight of her life, but instantly remembering the unborn fruit of their happy union, she repented of that impulse of despair, and cried out--

"No! do not heed my petition, O my God! I wish for life to dedicate it to the innocent babe which Thou hast given me to bear!"

Two months later Prudencia gave birth to a beautiful boy which cost its mother fearful suffering.

Eight years passed since Ignacio was born, and for these eight years the life of the mother had been one long chain of anguish and deep sacrifices to preserve the existence of that child who was born vacillating between life and death; but at length life triumphed, thanks to the mother's care.

"It is appalling to consider how much that child has cost you," used the pious hermit of San Bartolomeo de Berriz to say to Prudencia; "if there is a child in the world who ought to love its mother, it is most certainly your son."

On hearing these words Prudencia was unable to restrain her tears. Was it because her son did not love her as much as her love and great sacrifices deserved? Most undoubtedly it was.

There are few mothers who have not the right to call their children ungrateful! There are few sons who, after losing their mothers, do not feel in the depths of their hearts the remorse of not having loved them as much as they deserved!

Ignacio seemed to view with indifference the love and the tender solicitude of his mother whom he treated with disaffection, which in the unreflecting age of eight was not a very guilty act, but which nevertheless gave signs of that ingratitude and coldness of heart with which the son of Prudencia would repay the hapless mother her love and maternal solicitude and sacrifices. Up to his seventh year the child was reared weak and sickly, but on attaining this age his health began to improve wonderfully, and one year later he was one of the most robust, healthy children who frequented the shores of Ibaizabal. It was on the shores of Ibaizabal, and not on the heights of Goyerri, that Ignacio was to be found at all hours of the day, against the will of his mother; who feared that some misfortune would befall him on the water, but she in vain opposed his descent to the river.

Prudencia wished her son to become attached to the paternal home, to cultivate the land and the trees which surrounded it, and to pursue the agricultural pursuits of his country; but the water and boats and sailors were all in all the thoughts and love of the child. For him there was no field so beautiful as the wide expanse of the blue water, nor dwelling more lovely and desirable than a ship, nor society more agreeable than that afforded by the rough mariners, whose brows had become bronzed, and who had grown old wrestling with the tempest and fighting with pirates. Whenever his mother came to seek him in Olaveaga or Zorroz-aurre, she always found him exercising himself, rowing in a boat, or climbing a ship's mast, or playing on the deck of some vessel, or in the dingy alehouse frequented by the sailors, and where they met to spin their yarns, perfectly absorbed with the narrative of the adventures encountered by some crew.

If it had cost Prudencia many and dire sorrows to rear up her child, her trials were no less now when she beheld with dismay the growing love for the sea which he was daily manifesting.

The fond ambition of a mother can never be realized on beholding in her children the wish to leave their paternal home to seek the life of solitude and the constant perils of a life spent on the seas; and the ambition of Prudencia had been that her son should always remain at her side, cultivating the fields sown with patient love, and cheering the hearth around which so many tears had been shed by her.

Ignacio, on attaining his twelfth year, could read and write fairly well, thanks to his natural intelligence and the constant efforts of his mother to make him attend school, but certainly not due to his love of study. During the long winter evenings his mother insisted on his reading aloud books which were of a religious character, or such as recounted the history of the glories of the land of his birth; but the only book which Ignacio loved to read was a fantastic narrative of the voyages of Columbus, Elcano, and other navigators, and some romances, in which, for the amusement of the public, were related incredible accounts of maritime scenes which fired the imagination of that poor boy, who really seemed as though he had come into this world solely to torment and grieve his tender mother. The romantic and exaggerated narratives which the sailors daily recounted completed the pernicious effects produced by the injudicious reading he had pursued, on the vivid imagination of Ignacio. One day his mother bade him consider that he was already of an age to assist her in the arduous labour of cultivating the fields and tending the cattle. Ignacio to this replied, what his mother had long feared to bear, that he did not like the life of an agriculturalist, and he was firmly resolved to take to that of a sailor and proceed to sea.

90

In vain did Prudencia endeavour to dissuade her son from his resolve: the son insisted upon it; and thus the years passed until Ignacio completed his twentieth year, more and more decided upon exchanging the peaceful life, which was offered him by the surroundings of Monte Berriz, for the turbulent life of a seaman on the vast solitudes of the ocean.

The love of Prudencia for her son, in place of diminishing by the cold correspondence it met with from Ignacio, became, on the contrary, more ardent, deeper, more vivid, and firmer than it had ever been! Prudencia only existed to love God and her son. If any maternal love deserved the name of idolatry or madness, most assuredly it was that of this hapless mother.

III.

The pleadings and the tears of Prudencia did not suffice to deter Ignacio from his resolution of casting himself on the ocean, after a few limited voyages on the Cantabrian seas, which hitherto had only deprived Prudencia of his society for a few days. She felt she could not exist without him, and one day Ignacio ran up from the shore to impart to his mother the sad news that he had determined upon undertaking a voyage, which would be of some months' duration. And this was not the only resolution he had formed, and which he imparted to his disconsolate mother. He had decided that they should dispose of the house and land where his father had lived from his birth until he came to dwell in Aurrecoechea, and with the proceeds of the sale to purchase a beautiful swift ship which had been put up for sale on the shores of Zorroz-aurre. The tears and pleadings of his mother to deter him from doing this were met by Ignacio with his usual argument--that if he were to die a violent death, it would be just the same to meet it on the sea as on land, as had happened to his father, who met his death in the peaceful chestnut plantation of Goyerri.

Prudencia wrestled for a long time before she consented to the project of her son; but at length she was overruled; but what was most singular was the fact that, instead of acknowledging and understanding the selfish proceeding of her son, who was selling the paternal homestead and filling his mother with sorrow merely to gratify a caprice, her love, in place of growing weaker, became daily more strengthened as though it were fed by her abundant tears.

Some days after this, Ignacio, radiant with joy and pride, was directing the management of his ship, which had been manned and prepared for leaving the calm waters of Ibaizabal, whilst his mother was weeping unconsolably on the shore where a few moments previously her son had given her a cold farewell accompanied by these unfeeling words: "Come, come, we have had enough of this crying; good-bye for six months."

The ship slowly sailed away, carried along solely by the wind, because, as its master already considered himself quite a sea hero, he would not descend to the vulgar recourse of employing a towing rope! Prudencia did not remove her eyes, blinded by weeping, from watching the ship, waiting for the last sign of farewell of her son; but the ship disappeared behind the Monte del Sepulcro, without Ignacio remembering to turn to give one last look towards his disconsolate mother.

In those days there did not exist, as in our time, beautiful grassy acres along the plains of Elorrieta and Zorroz-aurre, which extended to the right of Ibaizabal from the Monte del Sepulcro to the white, well-populated district of Olaveaga, which then could only boast of a dozen houses, and what at the present day are fruitful lands and orchards, dotted by cheerful dwellings, was then sterile land overrun with rushes and washed by the waves.

With her heart torn asunder by grief, Prudencia crossed the place covered with bulrushes and reeds, and with slow steps ascended the slope of Goyerri, turning at every step to cast a look towards the north-west, seeking the ship which carried her son.

On reaching the chestnut wood of Aurrecoechea, she sought, as was her wont, for the tall chestnut tree, on the trunk of which was nailed a simple wooden cross, to shed a tear and repeat a prayer, and this day she cast herself on her knees close to the tree, and watered with her abundant tears the ground which had been steeped with the life-blood of her husband. This ground was on that occasion covered with flowers, and the blue hues of their petals seemed to be reminding her of the celestial Jerusalem wherein the All-powerful reserves unspeakable joys for the sad ones of this earth.

"Blessed are those that believe!" said Christ; and whereas Prudencia had faith and believed, she deposited there her sorrow on the breast of an Invisible Being. When she rose up from her knees to continue her walk to her sad, lonely home, she appeared quite comforted and freed from her great heavy burthen. On approaching her house she cast a last look behind. The sun, which was fast becoming hidden behind the mountains of the Encartaciones, was bathing with vivid rays the turbulent waters between Cape Lucero and Cape Villano, and, favoured by its resplendency, Prudencia distinguished and recognized her son's craft, and with eyes fixed on the ship she continued motionless until it disappeared in the mists of the evening.

Perchance the mother thought that at the same moment as she watched lovingly the ship, that fond eyes on board were full of tears, seeking amid the chestnut groves of Berriz for the white house of Aurrecoechea.

IV.

The plains which at the present day are known under the name of shores of Lamiaco were at the commencement of the seventeenth century called reed plantations, of Dondiz. Dondiz was the name of the cheerful, small village which stands on the green hills that overlook Lamiaco, and it was in this valley that an old man related to me the sad story of Prudencia, while he smoked his pipe and watched the herds pasturing on the grassy meadows.

In the Basque language, as also in Castillian, the name of Lamia implies one of the fantastic creations of the popular mind. Lamia is a class of water fairy which differs from a mermaid in this: that while the latter only dwells in the sea, and her singing allures men for evil, the former lives both in the sea and in the rivers, and her singing attracts men to them in order to render them happy.

To the bed of rushes on the shores of Dondiz was given the Basque name of "Lamiaco," which, literally translated, means the shores of the Lamia. "But why was this shore of Dondiz called Lamiaco?" We shall learn further on. In the seventeenth century those plains, which are at the present day fruitful lands, thanks to the industrial character of the people, and will soon rival the best cultivated acres of Biscay, were overgrown beds of dark rushes and dismal marshes, which the people believed were the haunts of monsters and wandering spirits.

But let us return to Prudencia. Nearly six months had elapsed since the departure of Ignacio, and the poor mother had received no tidings of him. In vain did she come down to Olaveaga and Zorriz-aurre every day, with the object of asking the sailors who returned from America for news of her son. No one could give her any tidings of Ignacio, nor of his ship. But as the term of six months had not yet expired of his absence when he had promised to return, Prudencia still had hopes.

"Should her son not return," said the hermit of San Bartolomeo, "what will become of poor Prudencia, who only lives because she expects her son to come back?

Prudencia would every day take the high road from the plains of Aurrecoechea, which skirts the southerly brow of Monte Berriz, and ends on the summits which are renowned in the modern history of Spain under the name of *Banderas*. Here she would stop and spend whole hours with eyes fixed on the ocean, always hoping to see on that vast sheet of moving waters the appearance of her son's ship, which she felt sure she could not mistake for any other. But the ship of Ignacio never appeared among the great number which daily passed the fearful line of swelling waves that extends from the broken rocks of Algorta to those of Santurce.

Her hopes began to wane when at the end of six months Ignacio had not returned. Yet Prudencia still continued every day to ascend to the summit of Berriz, to return more and more disappointed. In proportion as the poor mother lost hope her life visibly declined.

One afternoon she stood as usual on that height with eyes fixed on the far distant horizon. The sun was setting, inundating with light the gulf which extends between Capes Lucero and Villano, just as it had done on the day when the bark of Ignacio had crossed that water. Suddenly a white sail appeared in the far distance, lit up by the sun's rays, and Prudencia, uttering a cry of joy, descended the slope west of the Monte del Sepulcro, crossed the stream by a high narrow wooden bridge extending from the sombre tower of Luchana, crossed the plain and rocks of Aspré, and entered the reed marshes of Dondiz at the moment when the bark was saving the bar of Santurce. Prudencia had lost sight of the vessel behind one of the many peaks and rocks which hid it from her sight, but she continued to walk on along the shore, which was now comparatively dry owing to the low tide. Her heart beat wildly, her breathing was painfully laboured, while a feeling of anxious expectation was taking possession of her soul similar to that felt by the prisoner in a dungeon who knows that the first person to enter in is to bring him the sentence of death or liberty.

On coming out from behind a rock she suddenly found herself close to the much-longed-for ship, and, giving a cry of intense pain, she fell to the ground senseless, as though she had been struck down by a ray of lightning. Her heart and her eyes had deceived her. That ship before her was not the one of her son Ignacio. After some time she recovered consciousness, and, making a supreme effort, she sadly and slowly took the road to Ibaizabal as though she had lost the last hope which remained to her on earth.

When she reached Aurrecoechea the night was far advanced, and when the clock of the monks of Burceña struck twelve the soul of Prudencia left its earthly tenement, and was ascending to heaven.

V.

Further on than Aurrecoechea, almost on the summit of the mountain, there existed a beautiful hermitage dedicated to the apostle, Saint Bartholomew, and about the year 1379 some pious men, desirous of leading a life of prayer, and of sheltering the travellers who traversed those plains, which in those days were bereft of habitations and covered by dense forests, in which abounded many wild animals, joined themselves together and constituted a monastic order.

In 1429 the hermitage of Berriz was erected into a convent of Augustinians, and in 1515 the community removed to the neighbourhood of Bilbao, where the pious knight, Tristan de Leguizamor, gave them the land for founding their new house and for erecting a new church.

A century later--that is to say, in the first half of the seventeenth century--a pious woman took care of the hermitage of Saint Bartholomew, which has subsisted almost to our days, and this holy woman often participated in the troubles of Prudencia, and very frequently assisted her with wise counsels. The *nun of Berriz*, as this servant of God was called, had great fame for sanctity, and from her life of prayer and devout contemplation it was currently believed that her enlightened spirit could pierce the veils of the future.

At the moment when Prudencia breathed her last sigh, the nun of Berriz was kneeling in prayer before the holy altar of the apostle, and was favoured with a. singular vision. It seemed to her that the temple of Saint Bartholomew had disappeared from view, and that the gates of heaven stood in its place. She saw Prudencia surrounded by ineffable light and accompanied by a legion of happy mothers, whose love and maternal sacrifices had obtained for them the aureole of the saints, and was approaching to the throne of God, who spoke to her in this wise:

"Thou wast saintly as a daughter, as a wife, and as a mother; and because thou hast loved much and suffered greatly in the world, much eternal glory shalt thou have in heaven!"

"My God! I thank Thee!" cried Prudencia, smiling with ineffable joy, yet a tear glistened in her eyes.

"Dost thou perchance think this an insufficient reward for thy trials and sorrow?"

No, my God! for this is more than I deserve."

"Why, then, does a tear glisten in thine eyes?"

"Because there yet remains in me an atom of human weakness, and I am thinking that if my son returns to his native shores, there will be no one left to receive and welcome him!"

"I, who can do all things, will complete thy glory by dispelling in thy heart that last sorrow which binds thee to earth. Release that last atom of human nature from thy celestial nature, and, animated by thy holy motherly love, fly back to the shores of Dondiz!"

This brief dialogue concluded, the eyes of Prudencia, freed from the last earthly tear, shone with celestial joy because Prudencia was now one of the blessed, and no longer the earthly mother. And in an instant the strange vision disappeared from the sight of the nun of Saint Bartholomew.

A short time after this the people began to call the reed marshes of Dondiz, *Lamiaco*, because among its rush-beds commenced to be heard the singularly sweet song of Lamia, which is still heard, and will continue to be heard, as long as the sons of this land depart from its noble shores. The song of Lamia is heard whenever a ship leaves the waters of Ibaizabal to breast those of the ocean, and carries in her a child of its mountains. All the harmonies of the fatherland, beautified and glorified by the voice of angels, are united together in that song. The melody of the pipe and the timbrel which cheer the valleys; the songs with which our mothers and nurses lulled us to sleep in our cradles; the *zensuac*, the *ijuijac*, and *ujuju* of the mountaineers as they call each other from mountain to mountain, and from valley to valley. Their dreams, their martial joys, and their love anxieties; the song of the high road, and the murmur of the valley, and the noise of the windmill, and the hammers of the forge, which publish their industry. The ringing of their church bells, the thousand distant, lively rumours which wake up the plains and fields when feasts are held on festival days, the singing of the birds, the sighing of the breeze, and the roar of the sea waves as they dash against our coasts--in one word, all the melodies, all the songs, all the noises which constitute the breath, the life, the voice of the Basque existence, are united together in the song of the Lamia. And this song is sweet and alluring; and the ears that once hear it never can forget it; and the heart which beats on hearing it will never cease to beat for the fatherland towards which those who have departed far from it always yearn to return, because in their ears never ceases to resound the song of Lamia.

In course of time the house in which Ignacio was born, and where so many tears had been shed by his hapless mother, was converted into a convent of Capuchin Trinitarians, whose melancholy ruins I am beholding from the window of the room in which I am writing this; and it is a proud fact that the Venerable Father Matthias de Marguina, the first superior of that holy house, was in the habit of applying the holy sacrifice of the mass for the salvation of the son of Prudencia.

As regards the son of Prudencia, *he never returned, nor ever will return*, to his native shores, because God, whose justice finds a reward for all that is meritorious, and punishment for all that is evil, does not give to the monster who despises filial love the sweetest felicity of this earth--that of returning to the fatherland after he has sighed for it in his exile.

[1] *Lamia*. The Basque water-nymph, or mermaid.

THE VIRGIN OF THE FIVE TOWNS

"The vision approached nearer and nearer, and came and sat by the side of the sleeping woman and gazed upon him for a long time in silence."

The Virgin of The Five Towns

[1]

BALLAD.

AIRAM is sad, very sad; what ails Airam? An untiring huntsman, yet the aurora found him in Achular [2] with his bow slung over his shoulder and the faithful Bart lying at his feet. The thick branches of the trees of Esquiroz [3] sheltered his sleep from the burning rays of the sun, and the lasses of Sumbilla [4] rejoiced when, coming to the spring to draw water, they heard the merry songs of the youthful huntsman as he descended the declivity.

But now Airam is sad, very sad; what ails Airam? See him as he leans against the stone cross which divides Navarre and Aragon--his eyes fixed, his countenance pale, melancholy, and pensive.

Listen, stranger. Airam hunted all one day. At nightfall the damp beams of the white moon surprised him as he lay on the sward of Bardena Real. [5] The habitations were distant; the limbs of the huntsman were weary with fatigue, and he slumbered. And in his sleep he had a dream.

The pale moonbeams illumined an angelic form. It was that of a maiden of fifteen summers, dressed in white, like the ancient virgins of Carmel. The tresses of the vision were silky and as golden as the husk which pends from the maize when it is nearly ripe; her eyes were beautiful like those of the roe of Ollin: the face that of Benzozia, [6] the goddess of felicity and of chaste love. The heart of Airam palpitated visibly, a fierce fire devoured his soul. The young man placed his hand on his breast and found it empty. The vision approached nearer and nearer, and came and sat by the side of the sleeping huntsman, and gazed upon him for a long time in silence. The vision bent its head over the forehead of the youth, and the perfumed curls of the vision covered the face of the huntsman. Then in the mysterious silence of night resounded a kiss; then was heard a celestial voice, which arrested the course of the moon, and made its white beams flicker. It was a voice such as has not its equal on earth; a voice which arrests the fury of the hurricane as it is about to break over the heights of Canigou, [7] where it dwells; a voice which stills the waters against the promontory of Jaizquibel. [8] And she said:

"Airam! for two years have I sought you; from the lattices of my convent I have called you every night. The bark of your faithful Bart was echoed in the mountains, and the sound of your bugle-horn was lost in the distance. And I would return sadly and tearfully to my couch on perceiving that you heeded not my voice or my calls; and my companions mocked me in the morning because my eyes were swollen with weeping. Airam! Airam! my mouth calls you, my heart is breaking; come quickly, come, because else I shall lose you, and you me, for ever. I am Cingaya the Beautiful, I am the Virgin of the Five Towns."

The huntsman awoke with a start. The moon was placidly illuminating the greensward; his faithful Bart was sleeping quietly; the silence of that calm night was truly solemn; no figure or form appeared amid the fragrant bushes. Only on the road to Aragon, in the far distance, could be felt, rather than heard, the noise of a cavalcade approaching. The tramping of the horses grew louder. In front of this cavalcade rode the principal lord of Egea, of Sos, and of Verdun. At his side, seated on a white steed, rode a maiden, her face veiled by a silver gossamer, followed by a retinue of relations and friends and noble Aragonese pages.

"Tell me, good page, may Our Lady guard you. From whence come you?"

"From the neighbouring convent, gallant huntsman. Do you wish to know more? Make haste, then, for the cavalcade is departing."

"Tell me, good page, who is that maiden riding the white steed, and whose face is veiled in silvery gossamer?"

"She is our mistress: she is Cingaya the Beautiful, the Virgin of the Five Towns, who leaves her convent to be betrothed."

"Good page, tell me more; does Cingaya the Beautiful, the Virgin of the Five Towns, love her promised husband?

"She comes sad, gallant huntsman; sad and full of tears. Her promised husband is haughty and cruel; they wished to unite the fresh plant with the worm-eaten oak."

"Thanks, good page, thanks. Tell Cingaya the Beautiful that Airam the huntsman has his breast empty because his heart has gone after the Virgin of the Five Towns."

"It is too late," replied the maiden.

This is the reason, stranger, why Airam is sad; the reason why he leans against the stone cross, the bounds of Aragon and Navarre, his eyes fixed, his countenance pale, melancholy, and pensive.

Place, place to the minstrel who comes from distant lands! Place to him, for he comes in time to dispute the prize at the floral games. Clemencia Isaura [9] has made a sign to him; let us hear the stranger. And he commenced:

"Noble dames, listen with indulgence to the new rhymester: his voice is not sweet, because the hurricane of the Pyrenees, the tempest on the ocean, the simoom of the desert, have rendered his voice hoarse.

"I saw Zaira close to the cistern of Embrun; [10] Zaira was good and lovely. I am thirsty, I said to her, and she lifted her water pitcher, made of clay from the Nile, and put it to my parched lips."

"Love me, Nazarene, love me," she said, "for I love you. Around my tent wave the branches of twelve palm trees; I have twelve barns full of corn, and twelve camels of finest hair: love me, Nazarene!"

"You are not Cingaya the Beautiful, the Virgin of the Five Towns. She stole my heart while I slept on the sward: I cannot love you!"

"Allah be with you, good Nazarene. There lies the road to the West: you are right--I am less beautiful than Cingaya."

The new troubadour flung his cithern to his shoulder and embarked.

"I am Aimée, daughter of the deep; I am beautiful, as you see; I have necklaces of corals, bracelets of gold, girdles of morocco: love me, good minstrel, love me!"

"You are not Cingaya the Beautiful, the Virgin of the Five Towns. She stole my heart when I slept on the sward: I cannot love you!"

"God guard thee, good minstrel. From Cyprus to your land is a long journey. May love guide thee! You are right, I am less beautiful than Cingaya."

The new songster shouldered his cithern, and reached the land of his birth. Many years had passed since his departure.

"Where is Cingaya the Beautiful?" he asked the rocks of Achular. And the rocks replied, "She has departed from hence."

"Where is the Virgin of the Five Towns?" he asked the tree of Esquiroz. And the tree replied, "She has gone from here."

"Where is she who stole my heart while I slept?" he asked the sward of Bardena Real. And the wind sadly murmured also that she had gone away never to return.

Then the troubadour flung his cithern to his shoulder and came to Tolosa [11] to dispute the prize in the floral games. He will never return to his birthplace, to its mountains, because they have all told him that Cingaya the Beautiful had departed never to return.

"Noble dames, you have listened my voice is not sweet because the hurricane of the Pyrenees, the tempest of the ocean, the simoom of the desert, have rendered it hoarse."

Clemencia Isaura is shedding tears.

"How are you called good minstrel? Your ballad is a tender one, and your strange accent lends to it a greater value."

"They used to call me Airam the huntsman, but today I have no name."

"I will give you one, good minstrel. Behold, here is the golden rose, because you have nobly earned it. Sing, sing in your own beautiful language the glories of your warriors, sing the loves of the valleys, the hurricane of the mountains. The poet belongs to all the world; hence all true inspirations are drawn and felt only when close to the home which witnessed our birth."

Thus spoke Clemencia Isaura to the minstrel. The noble dame, veiled with the fine white gossamer, then approached the stranger.

"Have you still your breast empty and desolate?" she asked, deeply moved.

"Yes, noble dame, it is still empty."

"Take my heart, then, in place of yours. I am the vision of the sward of Bardena Real!"

The minstrel felt that his breast was filling with felicity.

"Yes, yes; you are Cingaya the Beautiful, the Virgin of the Five Towns," he said, clasping her in his arms.

Since that day never was Airam seen again leaning against the stone cross, the boundary of Navarre and Aragon, his eyes fixed in space, his countenance pale, melancholy, and pensive.

[1] *Five Towns of Aragon*. A group composed of the towns of *Sos, Sadava, Uncastillo, Tauste,* and *Egetz*--all situated on the frontiers of Aragon and Navarre, to the extreme of the Pyrenees.

[2] *Achular*. A mountain of Guipuzcoa, close to Andoain. There is another of the same name in the valley of Lerin, in Navarre.

[3] *Esquiroz*. A mountain situated in Navarre, on the confines of Bardena Real.

[4] *Sumbilla*. A lovely, picturesque town of Navarre, situated in the valley of Lerin, on the straight line with Vidassoa, about thirty-five kilometres from Pamplona.

[5] *Bardena Real.* A deserted arid plain cut through by rocks and broken boulders, extending from the junction of the rivers Ebro and Aragon to two kilometres beyond the frontier of the ancient kingdom of Aragon, a distance comprehending many kilometres.

[6] *Benzozia.* The Venus of chaste love of the primitive Basque people.

[7] *Canigou.* A high and inaccessible mountain of the French Pyrenees; part corresponds to Spain.

[8] *Jaizquibel.* A mountain which rises parallel to the Cantabrian Sea from the Port of Passagens to that of Fuenterrabia. At its extreme north there stood anciently the promontory of Olearso, in our days the Cape of Higuer.

[9] *Clemencia Isaura.* A noble lady descended from the nobles of Tolosa. She lived in the fifteenth century. It was she who revived in that city the famous floral games which had fallen into disuse for more than a century, and she left at her death, in 513, a fixed sum for defraying the expenses of those poetic tournaments.

[10] *Embrun.* A cistern situated in Palestine, and much renowned in the time of the Crusaders.

[11] *Tolosa.* The capital of the province of Guipuzcoa.

Kurucificatuaren Canta

[1]

(*The Chant of the Crucified.*)
BALLAD.

THE woods of Odolaga [2] are sombre from the abyss of Guesalza issue dismal sounds, and the Kuruceta [3] veils its face with a thick fog,

"Why do ye weep, maidens of Izaspi? [4] Why pluck your beards, ye ancients of Errazil? What mean these tearful eyes, and this disordered hair?"

No one replied to the stranger: sorrow has no words it is dumb like death. The maidens wipe away their tears; the ancients majestically enwrap their mantles around them, and sit down, deeply moved and silent, upon the broken-down trunks of their oaks. Yet though their sorrow may be immense and deep, the *Euscara* must not manifest himself weak to the eyes of the stranger. To others belong the loud plaints or the cry wrung from feeble spirits. The tree groans as it breaks down; the strong rock is cleft without hurting itself; the Euscara is like the rock--he dies; but without death being able to wrench from him a single sigh.

Out of the dense fog which is covering Kuruceta issues from its bosom sylvan harmonies and cries of triumph The Basque mountain is stirred to its base, and, shaking its granite front, flings to the winds its diadem of clouds. It is the full moon of May; the queen of night shows her sanguinary face towards Otsondo, [5] and with red beams illumines the mysterious heights. Sylvan melodies follow, and the cries of triumph become louder. The torrents stop their course; the winds of the forests become hushed, and timidly retire to take shelter amid the leafy branches. What mysterious sacrifice is about to be celebrated on the Basque mountain? Oh! what shadowy outlines rise up in the horizon! What a long line of lances! Nude bodies pend from upraised crosses; but the brows of the crucified are proudly lifted up; their looks are haughty, and their lips curl with contempt. Cries of triumph are uttered before the terrified Romans; the lips of the crucified are crying thus:

"Salve! moon of May, light of our feasts and of our lives! spread thy beams and encircle our brows with the brilliant crown of triumph and of martyrdom!"

"The Romans desire to see on our faces the contortions of agony; that is proper of cowards, and we are not cowards. These crosses are the thrones of our glory!

"They weep like children on yielding up their spirit we sing the song of death, the hymn of victory!

"Your Augustus Octavius is great, you say; and in truth he is great like yourselves--in pusillanimity and in treachery.

"Salve! May moon, which shines over fresh valleys, rugged mountains, and the shady woods of our land!

"Relate to our sons, to our wives, to our lovers, and to our country, the deeds of *Euscara* and the cowardice of the Romans who gaze on us.

"Tell them that we fling to the face of the son of the Tiber the blood which gushes from our wounds. Tell them that when our souls fly to heaven, our hearts will still continue to throb for our country!

"Satellites of the tyrant! land of slaves! We despise ye like the bear despises the fox; and on their faces, pale with terror, we hurl our contempt!

"Salve! thou moon of May, look at us well: we smile at pain; our countenances do not grow pale. The love of liberty and of our country still fills our hearts!

"Tell our beloved fathers and our dear brothers what you have seen; and that to the cries of triumph which resound from Kuruceta responds the cry of extermination and vengeance throughout the Basque mountains.

"May moon! light of May! kiss the brows of our children and of our mothers, and carry to our spouses, whom we received before the altar, the last throb of our hearts!

"Oh, May moon! repeat with us the last motto of our spirit, *Viva la Patria*! Hatred and contempt for idolatrous Rome!"

To this clamour replies another, great and echoing--terrible--a cry which fills the depths of the forests and fills the immensity of space. Then the Basque mountains remain silent; the woods of Odolaga become more sombre, and from the mouth of Guesalza [6] issues still more dismal sounds, and the Kuruceta veils her face with a more dense fog. And the beams from the May moon descends over the valleys, and consoles with its cold light the maidens of Izaspi and the ancients of Errazil.

[1] *Kurucificatuaren Canta.* (*The Chant of the Crucified.*) During the long and sanguinary war sustained by the Romans against the inhabitants of the Basque mountains, the prisoners who fell into the power of the Romans were crucified on the summit of the mountains with the object of inspiring the dwellers with terror. The heroic Basque people intoned while on the cross a chant of triumph and death, and also insulted their enemies, who witnessed with feelings of awe such manifestations of courage and lofty independence of spirit.

[2] *Odolaga.* A mountain which, forming a cordillera, separates the valleys of Baztan and Ulzama. It is covered with woods.

[3] *Kuruceta.* A mountain situated in Guipuzcoa and Navarre, upon which some hundreds of Basque prisoners were crucified during the wars against the Romans.

[4] *Izaspi.* An ancient place of Navarre.

[5] *Otsondo.* A mountain on the frontiers of France, near the Urdax, in Navarre.

[6] Guesalza. A cave of great depth and extension, full of crystals. It is situated near the Mondragon, in Guipuzcoa.

The Raids

"Houra! Cosacos del desierto, houra!
La Europa os brinda esplendido botin.
Sangrienta charca sus campiñas sean,
De los grajos su ejército festin."
--ESPRONCEDA.

("*Hurrah! Cossacks of the desert, hurrah! Europe offers ye a splendid booty. Bloody pools may her battlefields become, and vultures on her army feast.*")

SING, bard, sing! you who are as old as the world, and whose head began to whiten on the very day when the great beech of Berderiz [1] was planted. Sing, bard, sing! Eldest of our improvisatores; singer of our feasts, of our warlike deeds, of our loves! Sing a welcome to our brothers of the valley of Bertizarana, of Baztan, Of Aezcoa, of Erro, and of Roncal. [2] Salute with your most penetrative and sonorous "lecayo" our brothers of Elzupel, of Otsobide, Hernio, and Aitzgorri. [3]

The night is dark, and the wind whistles across the trees of Irati, [4] compelling the wolf of the mountains to hide its brown head. The night is darksome, and a whirlwind of snow is drifting the flakes in heaps. It is a pleasant night for us, children of the mountains and of the tempests. It is a night which terrifies the Roman matrons, and makes the sybarite son of the Tiber shudder as he ties on his soft couch.

We shall enter with strung bow into the gardens full of statues, into the palaces of marble, into the bedchambers hung with silken draperies. We must feast at the ivory tables, we must fill ourselves with the wines of Syracuse and of Cyprus, quaffed in cups of gold and precious stones. Our women will work mantles of purple--standards to serve as guides in the battles--and will plait their hair with threads woven with the silver of their cups. The chieftain of the frontiers on hearing the "irrinzi" will mistake it for the noise of the hurricane, and we shall traverse the plains swift as the winds. The Romans crucified our prisoners, and we must devastate their cities and tread down their fields. And by the light of the conflagrations our sons, crowning the crests of the mountains, will intone hymns of victory.

Sing, bard, sing! This is the hour of our raid: the owl screeches in the crevices, the wolf hides in the caverns, the eagle, timorous, thrusts its beak under the wing; because night is fearful to all creatures, save to us, sons of the mountains and of the tempest. Come, brothers, forward! We drink our last wine, and eat our last bread, and our children ask for more! Reach the cup of sour milk, and let us drink our parting cup. Forward, my sons! Let our women sleep, and hush our mastiffs. The raid will last eight suns.

Thus spoke the chieftain of Izalzu, [5] and great acclamations resounded among the rocks of Orbara, [6] and the torrent, which later on took the name of Irati, stayed its rapid course.

An hour later, and the mountaineers traversed the deserted parts of Montlig and Astarac. [7] To the right appear, like so many skeletons of gigantic elephants amid the shades of night, the Druidical altars of Asté, Sem, Nestos, and Heas. [8] From thence they descend and sally out of the darksome defiles of Zulogaraya, Izotzce, and Asarosta, [9] into the fertile plains of Novempopulania. [10] They descend silently and sinister, like the black, immense wave, the first breath of the hurricane which at night surprises the heedless ship.

Novempopulania slumbers in the midst of gardens and flowers, its splendid palaces built of the marble of Paros and of gold from Ethiopia, and out of them exhales, from among their peristyle columns, the perfumes of the feasts of night. And they descend, those sons of the mountains, like bands of water birds, enveloped in the dismal mantle of the tempest. The watch-guards of the Roman fortresses are showing their bare heads and, flinging aside their lances, sleep at will; because the mountain is far distant--because no noise comes from thence--because the storm increases, and the night continues fearful and darksome. The waters of the Adour and of the Nive [11] are filled with the multitude that are swimming across silently, The neigh of the warhorse is not heard; nor is the red standard of the *Three Hands* waving in the air; nor is the echo awakened by the "irrinzi" of war.

Virgins of Leheren, of Iscilo, and Arai, repose peacefully. Only can your sleep be agitated by the great voice of the tempest, or by the last chords which vibrate from the citherns of gold. Nevertheless, during your waking hours you will smile at the image of the patrician who subjugated the heart, wearing on his brow the diadem of triumph in the Hypic games! And you will do well; because the mountain is distant, and no noise comes from thence; because the storm increases, and the night is fearful and darksome.

Towards the furthest compass of the horizon is seen a red point; another here and there, and some nearer. Oh, how these luminous points increase! How do the waters of the rivers seethe! What clamours are mingled in the roar of the tempest! What shadows are those which glide along the vast plains? What smoke is that which rises like a funereal pall, and interposes between earth and the firmament?

Sing, bards, sing! Sing the incursions of the sons of the mountains and of the tempest! The lances are dripping with blood; the men come loaded with spoils. Sing, bard, sing! May your sonorous voice be echoed across the woods and forests of Cahella, of Belaya, and of Ahaide, [12] singing the victory of the sons of Aitor. Sing, bard of the silvery beard! Our children will have white bread and red wine until they are satiated, and our chieftains crucified in Kuruceta and Izascun smile from within their sepulchres.

The son of the Tiber remains there below, amid the ruins of the burnt-out palaces. Next spring the lime-tree of pale yellow flowers will cover the devastated gardens.

Farewell, my brothers, farewell! In our next incursion we shall swim across the Ebro, and our war-cry will reach even to Moncayo.

[1] *Berderiz*. A mountain situated at two kilometres from the town of Irurita, in the valley of Baztan.

[2] *Bertizarana*, &c. Valleys of Navarre, on the frontiers of France. The three first are narrow and surrounded by very high mountains.

[3] *Elzupel*, &c. Mountains. The two first belong to Navarre and the third to Guipuzcoa.

[4] *Irati*. One of the principal mountains of Navarre. It is covered by dense woods, in which are found lynx, bears, wolves, and all kinds of large game. The circumference of the base of this mountain is about fifty kilometres. One part belongs to France, and the rest to Navarre.

[5] *Izalzu*. A village situated five kilometres from Ochagabia, in the valley of Aezcoa, in Navarre.

[6] *Orbara*. A precipitous defile of the valley of Aezcoa, in Navarre.

[7] *Montlig* and *Astarac*. Deserted places of the French Pyrenees.

[8] *Asté*, *Sem*, *Nestos*, and *Heas*. Mountainous and deserted places in the centre of the Pyrenees.

[9] *Zulogaraya*, &c. Defiles or passes of the French Pyrenees, which have their commencement in Spanish territory.

[10] Novempopulania. During the epoch of the domination of the Romans this district extended from the Cantabrian Ocean to the margin of the river Garona, and from the first slope of the French Pyrenees to the margin of the above-said river and its mouth into the sea, forming an acute angle.

[11] *Nive*, &c. A French river, which springs on the declivity to the north of the Western Pyrenees, and joins the river Adour in Bayonne, and jointly flows into the Cantabrian Ocean.

[12] *Cahella*, &c. High and very luxuriant mountains, close to the valley of Roncal, in Navarre.

The Holy War

BALLAD

It is the autumnal equinox. The hurricane sweeps with potent breath the leaves of the olive and the vine in the provinces of the south, and directs its course, howling, towards the Basque mountains. The night is dark; the woods of Biscay, the precipitous cliffs of Guipuzcoa, and the and plains of Alava, are full of those tremendous echoes which appal the manliest spirit. The homesteads and granges are stirred to their foundations; the lofty chimneys are shaken; and the proud chestnut which grows near the doors shake their branches in a furious manner as though engaged in a noble wrestling with the wind. The hurricane continues its unbridled march. On meeting with the boulders of rocks overtopping the mountains, it seems to wish, in its fury, to wrench them suddenly, and cast them wrathfully down; and then, turning round in its impotent rage, encircles the huge bulks with mighty spirals of whirlwinds; and on witnessing how futile are all its efforts, it casts itself headlong, roaring, into the valleys. Then to that fearful noise is mingled the pitiful cries of nature assailed and beaten.

The *Echeco-Jauna* [1] sleeps peacefully, as well as his faithful mastiff, without being disturbed by those dismal howlings so familiar to the sons of the mountains and of the forests. The mastiff, however, suddenly raises its enormous head, pricks up its ears, opens its jaws, and utters a howl of alarm. The echeco-jauna lifts his head, and, leaning his elbow on the bed pillow, lends attentive ear, and with feverish hand grasps the bugle of war.

What was it awoke the echeco-jauna? And what alarmed the mastiff? Amid the howlings of the tempest a great voice was heard: this voice resounded from beyond the Ebro. It was the cry of a whole people offended in its dignity and stained in its honour.

Thus did our Basque chieftain and his faithful mastiff interpret that cry. They both ascended the summit of the mountains, and to the roaring of the tempest is quickly added the sound of the bugle of war.

All at once huge flames shoot up along the entire chain of mountains from Larum, the frontier of Navarre, to Tolosa, the frontier of Castile. And the echoing sound of the war-bugle rises above the noises of the storm, flies across the woods of Biscay, along the precipices of Guipuzcoa, and sweeps the arid plains of Alava. And the chieftains of the three tribes, from the heights of Gorbea, [2] Amboto, [3] and Aitzgorri, [4] repeat unceasingly the war cry, floating the standards of war lashed by the tempest. From Gorbea, from Amboto, and from Aitzgorri issue the call which no Basque ever leaves unanswered.

Ia, ia, ia, ó, ó, ó! Bill-Zaar, in Vitoria, in Tolosa, and in Guernica! [5]

And this call vibrated throughout the whole Euscuara [6] nation, who replied with tremendous vehemence: "Ia, ia, ia, ó, ó, ó, bill-zaar, bill-zaar!"

105

"Rise up from your sepulchres, ye warriors and bards of historic times! Shake off the funeral dust of ages; tear asunder the grave-clothes, ye Zurias, ye Ayalas, ye Lavas, and thousands of other heroes of ancient Euscarian epic poetry! Hasten to attend the 'bill-zaar' of Biscay, of Guipuzcoa, and of Alava. Your descendants have not yet become degenerate; there you will hear from mouth to mouth the motto of your ancient shields--*Ill, edo guaraitu!*"

"In what are you engaged, illustrious Alavese matron?"

"In broidering for my son, who goes to the Holy War, this blessed scapular of Our Lady ad Nives."

"And you, beautiful Bergarese maiden, what work are you doing?"

"I am working for the idol of my heart, who is proceeding to the Holy War, the scapular of Our Lady of Aránzanzu."

"What work is that which so occupies you, noble daughter of Durango?" [7]

"I am busy making a scapular of the Virgin of Begoña for my beloved brother to wear as he goes to the Holy War."

"And do you know where your son and lover and brother are going to, noble Basques?"

"Listen, stranger: they are going across Spain, as in the ancient days they crossed Gallias; they are going to pass the strait, as they formerly passed the Rhodano; they are going to utter their cry of war and victory from the heights of Atlas, as they once did on the plains of Capua. They are going to assist their brothers of Castile; they are going to wash out the affront which stains the face of our common mother; they are going to die or conquer as they did in Regil, [8] as in Cannas, [9] as in Covadonga, [10] and as in Navas.

"Do you see, stranger, those three diaphanous clouds which float on the horizon? They enclose the souls of the ancient heroes who died for their country. Do you hear the sweet melodies which pierce the winds? They are the voices of those who are praying to God for the victory and triumph of their descendants. Do you perceive the wide ray of light which illumines the whole Euscuara land? It is but the dim reflex of the brilliant aureole which crowns the glorious brows of those who die for their God, for their country, and for their king.

"Our war flags, our standard of the Three Hands shall wave by the side of the glorious flag of Castile, and then, alas! for the standard of Mahomet!

"Should our sons perish, there yet remain ourselves to avenge their death. If our sons die, their souls will ascend in diaphanous clouds, intoning hymns to God, their glorious brows crowned with aureoles which will far exceed the sun in brightness."

Thus spoke the illustrious dames and maidens of the Basque provinces.

"May you be blessed of God one and a thousand times, noble women!" replied the stranger, and then disappeared.

"Come, sons of the mountains! Rise up like one man to the sound of the hymn of war and liberty! Thirty ages of combats and victories have distinguished the three tribes of the Pyrenees and cast over them a splendour--a splendour which has never been dimmed of its pristine glories.

"Sus, sons of Aitor, the famous and enlightened founder of our progeny! Go, for your brothers from beyond the Ebro are calling ye. Grasp with powerful arm the victorious weapon, and march towards Africa, with your noble faces lifted up, your looks haughty, and your countenances calm. March towards Africa, and may your war-whoop shake the Atlas! There do new combats await you and new triumphs. Wrestle until you die against your enemies, and God grant that your glory may ever shine brightly like the flames of the three lamps in the feasts of the mysterious!"

Thus spoke the Basque chieftain; and three powerful armies replied to the spirited call, and ran to the combat amid the frenzied acclamations of a whole nation, who cried out:

"Ia, ia, ia, ó, ó, ó, ill edo garaitu."

[1] *Echeco-Jauna*. The head of the family, proprietor, &c.
[2] *Gorbea*. A mountain of Alava, which overlooks the plains upon which stands the city of Vitoria.
[3] *Amboto*. A very high cliff situated on the frontiers of Guipuzcoa, Alava, and Biscay.
[4] *Aitzgorri*. Mountain of Guipuzcoa: a continuation of Aloña. It rises 1·800 metres above the level of the sea.
[5] *Guernica*, *Arriaga*, and *Guerekiz*. The three camps where in ancient times were gathered together the *bill-zaars*, or meetings of the ancients. The first was in Alava, the second in Biscay, and the third in Guipuzcoa.
[6] "*Euscuara*, or *Euscara*. The name given by the Basque to those who speak it." See Essay on the Basque Language, by M. Julien Vinson, in "Basque Legends," by the Rev. Wentworth Webster.
[7] *Durango*. Principal town of Biscay.
[8] *Regil*. The ancient Errazill. A town close to Tolosa, of Guipuzcoa. Its inhabitants routed the Romans in the time of Augustus.
[9] *Cannas*. A celebrated battle gained by Hannibal against the Romans. A vanguard of the Carthaginian army which decided the victory was composed of Basque auxiliaries.
[10] *Covadonga*, *Navas*, and *Salado*. Three famous sanguinary battles, in which the Moors were routed: in these the Basque legions took an active part.

The Prophecy of Lara

[1]

BALLAD

ON the height of the Aloña, [2] in the district of Oñate, rose up a noble edifice of marvellous construction. In that rugged land, far from all human habitation, one day appeared before the astonished gaze of Rodrigo de Balzétegui a beautiful maiden amid the thorny bushes, to whom the shepherd in surprise asked, "Aránzan, zu?" [3] The first shelter erected for this maiden was a rustic thatch made of leaves. Towards the end of the sixteenth century this rude hut was converted into the building which forms the subject of this ballad.

The convent, as well as the river which has its rise in the neighbourhood, bears for its appellation the simple question of the shepherd to the maiden Aránzanzu. Any one on beholding that convent [4] would say that it must have been erected in the air by some powerful genius, and when concluded was placed on the sharp points of the rocks on the summit of the mountain. So bold was its construction that it appeared to be the work due to some supernatural agency, and not the work of man. Its immense body sustained by arches, extended from cliff to cliff, and across the aerial foundations, could be seen the firmament from one side, and on the other the fearful chasm known by the name of "*Leap of the Devil;*" while on its highest and most inaccessible point rose up the august symbol of our holiest religion.

One night I found myself leaning against a rock on the shore of the river Aránzanzu. To the right, and on the opposite side to the small valley, rose up in the distance the mountain and town of Urréjola, like an eagle's nest perched on the sharp point of a rock. Almost in front, in the distance also, and at the base of a deep and fearful precipice, could barely be distinguished across the mist the village of Arraoz imbedded in the crags like the diamond in the mines of Brazil. Throughout space, as far as the eye could reach, no other human habitation could be perceived. Rocks and broken cliffs on all sides, covered with a stunted vegetation, leaving the sharp broken heights bare. Some vulture of heavy flight would pass the night on the mountains to digest in perfect quietude its nauseous food which perchance it had grasped in the morning on the fertile Andalusian plains. Other birds of prey would conceal themselves screeching in the fearful cavern of St. Elias, which, according to tradition, is so deep that its termination has never been found. The limpid, seething, running waters of Aránzanzu flowed on--that stream which had its rise buried in the abyss and carried along through a wide defile, to come out again at a distance and pay its tribute to the river Deva; an image of frivolous youth which hides itself joyously in the abyss of old age and pays its tribute to death. This rugged landscape was illumined by the beautiful moon of May which, suspended in space like a lamp, diffused its damp silvery beams over the land. The sudden transition from light to shade brought out more vividly in relief the rude points of the cliffs; and on observing so many crevices, such thick brushwood, so deep a silence, such a marvellous calm, one would fain have said that all that space had been a vast sea which, rising up, agitated by the force of an equinoctial hurricane, into huge crested waves, had suddenly become petrified at the signal of the Supreme Creator; or else, some fabulous city peopled by giants which had become instantly ruined by an immense cataclysm. And, in truth, I saw--and let it not be doubted--enormous ruins of fallen walls, half-ruined towers of some unknown architecture, which still preserve ramparts and loopholes, columns and fantastic arches, in the ruins of which could not be discovered any vestiges of architectural rules either ancient or modern.

What had all this been in the primitive ages? Into what will it be converted when the consummation of ages comes?

I was dwelling on all this, and my restless imagination transported itself back to remote epochs and to other ages. In the darksome depths of those precipices and chasms, I saw, rising up slowly, masses of snow, white and transparent, which by degrees were acquiring vague forms, ending by appearing to my astonished eyes like human forms. Venerable old men with long white beards, and clothed in the rich dalmatics [5] of the primitive Basques, silently passed before me in an orderly procession, and directed towards me sad looks, then continued their aerial march in the direction of the solitary convent of Aránzanzu. Behind these, and in the same order, followed young warriors with naked swords in their right hands, while many of them had their left hands pierced by nails. These were the legions which, under the command of Hannibal, gained the battle of Cannas. And there were also the soldiers who had died crucified by the Romans, intoning on the cross the hymn of death. There were there those brave warriors who for the space of five years had wrestled alone and without support against the Roman legions when the empire was at its height, and were commanded by the most fortunate general of that epoch. Martyrs of Kuruceta, Iturrioz, and Altobicar! heroes of Cannas, Regil, and St. Adrian! As such did I salute those venerated shadows which passed before me. At their head marched Lara, the famous Guipuzcoan warrior, and more renowned still as a bard. His brow was crowned by the green diadem of yew leaves, and in his hand he carried a musical instrument of an unknown make. The same sad look was directed to me by the second procession as it passed before me, following the march of the ancients who had already disappeared. Then issued a long line of matrons and maidens, the latter distinguished by their long flowing hair; of children of both sexes, who, silent and sad, with eyes bent to the ground, and arms crossed over their breasts, were following the steps of the youthful warriors. At short intervals succeeded other processions, in which were seen the heroes of Covadonga, Navas, and Salado: the Canos, the Urbietas, the Oquendos, the Churrucas, and many more. Behind, and as though closing the march, came a dense black cloud, in the centre of which could be discovered a wide empty space which was radiant with light.

That procession was a magnificent living epic poem. Those who walked in it were men of bygone ages. Within the empty luminous space in the centre of the dark cloud which enveloped the huge procession, was there perchance any place for the men of future ages? Where did these shadows proceed to? What signified that marvellous silence and those sad looks? Do they perhaps see looming in the future the ruin of the country?

I rose up as soon as they were lost to view and continued my journey. The same peacefulness, the same silence in nature. From time to time there reached my ears, amid the breezes, the noise of running water, or the sad echo of the cry of agony of a gull, surprised in its nest by some bird of prey.

On reaching one of the angles of the path I followed, and from whence can be discovered the convent of Aránzanzu, I noticed with surprise that the shadows which I had seen passing before me, now occupied the summits of the pointed rocks which on every side surround the building. The white robes and rich dalmatics in which some were robed, the brilliant corselets and the coats of mail with which others were covered the flowing garments of the women and children, imparted to that numerous assembly which, motionless mustered together, had taken possession of the pointed heights, a fantastic appearance impossible to describe, I stood there in presence of that strange spectacle. The silence of nature was unbroken, the immobility of the shadows suffered no change.

Suddenly, he who stood on the cliff called the "leap of the devil," raised his hand, and a soft melody spread through space.

All the shadows knelt down. It was a novel scene. The scenery was the primitive landscape; the musicians and singers were invisible; the auditory was composed of the venerated shadows of our ancestors. The music which reached my ears was solemn, without ceasing to be melodious; the torrent of harmony which, beating against the rocks, became lost in distant echoes, was not similar to that which is usually heard in the temples. It was a strange harmony, a singular music executed with instruments hitherto unknown, sung by voices which had nothing human in them.

Wailings were heard which made one shudder, plaints that deeply moved the soul, sighs which rent asunder the heart; and then succeeded soft airs, melodious hymns that seemed to distil into the spirit a comfort such as no doubt is reserved for the just. And all this joined together, united, interlaced with each other, in harmony like to an enormous concerted piece accompanied by vigorous instrumental power of sound, while at times it vibrated in tender modulations and became sweetly sentimental.

The eolian harps of northern countries, accompanying the canticles of Ossian, did not possess the charm with which I listened enraptured. At the moment when the moon was hiding behind the top of Aitzgorri, and simultaneously as the shadows of the ancient Guipuzcoans were disappearing, the melodies which had ravished my spirit also began to lose their vigour. And by slow degrees these sounds died away, until the moon became completely hidden, and the fantastic shadows disappeared also, and the music ceased in a prolonged sweet chord.

Suddenly the magnificent scene was changed: the light succeeded to the darkness, and to the melodies followed the screech of the nocturnal birds. At that very instant I felt an icy cold hand placed on my head. I raised my eyes in terror, and I saw Lara the warrior prophet, the Basque bard, who was gazing on me with melancholy looks. A nimbus of soft light surrounded the manly head, crowned with a circlet of yew leaves. Over his tunic of finest white wool glistened a splendid dalmatic, the symbol of authority. In his left hand rested a stringed instrument of a make unknown to me. A sad smile hovered around the pale lips of the bard. After looking at me for some time in silence, he said, in a very sweet voice:

"Sit down and listen, my son."

I mechanically obeyed, and had hardly sat down when the wasted fingers of the prophet began to strike the chords of his singular instrument, producing plaintive sounds similar to the sighing of a dying child. Then, fixing his eyes on the firmament, commenced to issue from his lips murmurs which at first were unintelligible, but which later on made themselves clear to my attentive ear.

"The time flies, the torrents descend, the waters of the river flow on, following their course," said the prophet.

When listening to this allegory and simple exordium I imagined I perceived in the shadow of the bard the image of Aitor, the ancient of ancients, the patriarch, the father of the Indu-Atlantic race, the first and most perfect of Basques.

"The men of my race," he continued, "populated Hispana covered with a parasite vegetation; and that virgin soil was cleared of those plants by means of fire. The immense flames were reflected on the ice of the north, and their wide columns of smoke obscured the clear sky on the margins of the Ganges."

"Then we were happy and free."

*   *   *   *   *   *

Innumerable hordes of strange people, attracted by the gold which we despised, overran Hispana. We abandoned the plains to those avaricious merchants, and we retired to the mountains to follow our pure and holy customs.

"We were then still happy and free."

*   *   *   *   *   *

The sons of Romulus arrive; the masters of the world invade the plains. The Basque chief ascends the top of the mountain, and his 'irrinzi' of war moved the waters of the Tiber, which takes refuge in the Betica to hide its confusion,

"We were even then happy; we were still free, while all the countries of the world were following fettered to the triumphal car of a Roman Cæsar."

*   *   *   *   *   *

"What rumours are those which come from all the points of the horizon? What savage cries are those which thus disturb the peace of the Basque home? Does perchance the icy wind of the north bring in its wings the sombre and malevolent genii of the snowy regions?

"Populous and magnificent cities become a prey to the flames, lofty towers are hurled down, strong rampart walls fall to the earth. Whole nations disappear like sparks which the wind carries away, when passing through them, that multitude of people dressed in skins, of ferocious countries, who came uttering vociferous cries of death and extermination.

111

"Nevertheless we were still happy and free, because the swaying of that multitude becomes broken up and dashed to pieces against our haughty mountains."

* * * * * *

"This time is heard the sound of clarions and Moorish drums, the half-moon glistens on green standards, dark faces populate the plains, the call of the Muezzin takes the place of the sonorous tinkle of the bells.

"Alas for Spain! Her inhabitants bend their necks beneath the yoke of the Agareni!

"The tempest came from the south on this sad day.

"However, on this occasion also the African tribes retreat their invading march on beholding the Basque flag floating from the heights of Amboto.

"And even then we were still happy, because we were free."

* * * * * *

"But since that day many years and ages have passed away."

* * * * * *

The bard hushed his voice. His eyes suddenly acquired an extraordinary light; over his countenance was spread an expression of undefined wrath; the chords of his instrument vibrated with greater power, and the voice of the prophet, sonorous, terrible, clove the air extinguishing the sighing of the night wind, and increasing like the moaning of the river.

"Still more dangers for the country!" he cried. "Yes, see there the castles and the lions! see them disposed to oppress this ancient and free home with their threats! Numerous hordes are formed beyond the Ebro.

"Yes, hear them proclaiming a false liberty--they wish to deprive us of ours!"

* * * * * *

"Eia! sons of Aitor, ye who have sustained thirty ages of combats for your liberty and independence!

"Eia! unearth your arms, and utter the ancient formidable war cry!

"Eia! The shadows of our brothers are also joined on the camps of Arriaga, Guernica, and Guerekiz, to ask the God of battles help and protection as we now meet together to implore assistance from the holiest virgin of Aránzan-zu!"

After saying this the eyes of the prophet lost their light; his brow grew sad, and he remained silently bending down to the ground. And from his pale lips issued these words:

"What force cannot obtain, craftiness and bad faith will effect. Farewell, my son; the country is perishing and to my noble race nothing remains but bitter weeping."

He placed his icy hand on my head, and, gradually vanishing away, disappeared mingled with the shadows of the night.

* * * * * *

Four months later the Basque provinces had risen up, and all its sons were hastening to the war. This war lasted seven years, and was ended by an embrace. The great Basque chieftain died in front of his army. Peace be to his soul! The sanctuary of Aránzanzu fell a prey to the flames.

Should any one attain to behold the grand scene which I have roughly depicted, he will most certainly see, in the luminous centre of the dense cloud which closed up the march of the procession of shadows, surrounded by a brilliant aureole, and with hands joined--Jáuregui, [6] the shepherd-hero of the war against Napoleon, and Zumalacarregui, [7] the hero of the seven years' war. In the temple of glory there is no entrance for political passions. Beyond the camp there is bliss and peace for the good alone.

[1] *Lara.* A young bard and Basque chief of the period when the wars were raging against the Empire of Rome. The poet, Silio Italico, in the sixteenth book of his Epic Poem, assigned a whole page to describe the personal combat of Lara against Scipio, in which the Basque chief lost his right hand.

[2] *Aloña.* A mountain of Guipuzcoa, at whose southerly base is situated the magnificent town of Oñate, where, for a long period during the seven years' civil war, the Infante Don Carlos de Bourbon, uncle of Isabella II., held his court.

[3] *Aránzan, zu.* Literally, "You, in a thorn?"

[4] Convent of Aránzanzu. Situated on the south-west skirt of the Monte Aloña. The convent was under the invocation of Our Lady of Aránzanzu, and was inhabited by the friars of the Order of St. Francis. The situation of this convent was very remarkable. It was perched, so to say, on the highest point and most rugged and bare of the mountain, on the height of a steep declivity, and from this may be inferred the boldness and solidity of that capricious construction. Throughout the three Basque provinces the holy image of Our Lady of Aránzanzu was very famous, and the devotion of the people to it, even in our days, very general. During the month of May it is visited by numerous pilgrimages, and nothing more fantastic can be imagined than the effect produced by the glare of the fires at night, which are lit by the multitudes encamped on the mountain, as they are unable to find accommodation for all in the spacious inns close to the convent, and to hear the echoes of the magnificent organ, harmonious orchestra, and large choir of voices, with which they celebrate the praises of the Virgin and intoned the prayers. The convent was only visible at the distance of about fifty metres. I am sorry to add, that this singular construction was set fire to by orders of General Rodil during the civil war against Don Carlos--a deed of barbarism which will always merit reprehension and condemnation.

[5] *Dalmatic.* A very rich robe embroidered with gold spangles, worn over tunics of white wool on great festivals by the ancient Euscaros in olden times. This dalmatic was used as a sign of authority. The shape of this robe is exactly as the vestments worn during High Mass by the officiating deacon and sub-deacon, with the sole difference that the dalmatic has a hood. The "capusay" of the shepherds and country people of our time, worn in the Basque country, is an exact copy of that very ancient robe.

[6] *Jáuregui (Gaspar).* Field-marshal in the service of the Queen D. Isabella II. He was a native of Villa-real, of Guipuzcoa. He had been a shepherd, and during the war against Napoleon was an untiring guerilla chief.

[7] *Zumalacarregui* (*Thomas*). A native of Ormaiztegui, in Guipuzcoa. He was general-in-chief of the army of Don Carlos. He died from the effects of a wound received in the first siege of Bilbao, in 1835. He was one of the best Spanish generals of this century.

Hurca-Mendi

[1]

IRANZU! IRANZU! where are you going to, running, speeding along the rugged heights of Sorazu, leaping brake ferns and broken cliffs? Perchance, has the fearful *irrinzi* of war resounded along the defiles of the Urola, or have the heights of Mauria been enkindled with the foreboding bonfires, the sight of which makes, the hearts of mothers and maidens shudder with terror? No, no; your hands do not grasp the warlike bow, nor from your shoulder pends the quiver full of arrows, poisoned with the sap of the *tejo*! You are not going to the combat, Iranzu! The sons of your race enter the battle-field with a song, and they fall calm at heart. Their gaze is free of fear or dread, but to-day your eyes are sombre like the night, and your heart is agitated like the tempest when it rages amid the woods. You suffer and weep! Down among the chestnuts of Artadi is likewise seen a maiden, sweet like hope, beautiful as bliss, and she sighs sadly on murmuring your name. Iranzu! Iranzu! why did you go to the *Gara-paita* [2] of Artadi if your life was passing calmly and happily dwelling in the ancient homestead of your elders? Have you not heard, at times, that shadows of sadness and mourning obscured the fate of your child?

One day, when that lovely child, a babe, still in her cradle, was placed beneath the oak tree which shaded the doorway, an aged *Astiya* [3] passed by, and stayed to gaze upon that child with deep emotion.

Suddenly her eyes were filled with tears, and her tremulous lips murmured with sad accents a name. It was the name of her child--her child which she had lost that moon, and its memory had made her heart of mother shudder rudely! Because even the *Astiyas*, when they are mothers, have loving hearts and feel affection towards those little ones whom they have borne!

Touched tenderly by the memory of her lost one, she endeavoured to imprint a kiss on the fresh, rosy cheek; but the innocent babe repelled with dread and fear her kisses and caresses. The vengeful *Astiya* spitefully uttered over her brow mysterious words of cursing and death!

Have none of those words reached to you, Iranzu? Listen, listen. "May a curse fall on the first youth who shall make your heart beat, and receives your first kiss of love!" she hissed.

And you are the first, Iranzu, who has attained to agitate the mind of that maiden; you the first who has made her virgin soul tremble with love; you who have won her loving caresses! Unhappy one! Better had it been for you had you encountered on the mountains of Otoso a herd of famished wolves, than have met the blue eyes of the maiden of Artadi! How could you dream of obtaining the hand of that rich heiress, you, poor cadet of Biscay, who has for his only heirloom *a tile, a tree, and coat of mail*? [4] Fly from her, Iranzu! Forget that perchance she is waiting for you at her window, listening with beating heart for the sound of your footsteps!

But alas! the son of Iranzu will not turn back, because he is love-stricken, and he will not return until he has seen her, even should he have to leap across the black mouth of the chasm of Aitz-belz, [5] which descends, down to the bottomless pit. He runs, runs, and at length he reaches Artadi. Oh, how his heart beats on quitting the shades of the trees which overshadow her window! Oh, how he trembles and shudders as by the light or the moon he discovers the sweet brow of the love-stricken damsel!

But she is sad. Her eyes are swollen with tears, her looks reveal much anguish, her cheeks are pale! It is because the angel of pain, on passing swiftly, has left on her lips a kiss of death.

"What ails you, dove of Artadi?" cries the youth, with impassioned accents.

HURCA MENDI.

*"And wrenching off the splendid crown which encircled its brow
he precipitately ran out of the church."*

"Iranzu?" she murmured.

"You are weeping! What is the matter?"

"Fly from hence, Iranzu!"

"What do I hear?"

"Oh, I hear my father coming--retire, Iranzu. But, first, one word. The *Eche-jaun* of Igueldo has asked for my hand!"

"Oh! and what have you replied? What does your father say?"

"My father has accepted him, and I------"

"You vacillate?"

"What am I to do? He is my father."

"He is your father, 'tis true. But I--I am your lover; oh, tell me--do you love me? If so, come with me! fly with me! Come, I will give you my heart and my life. I will win for you riches and a name!"

115

"It is impossible, Iranzu!"

"Oh! but listen to me!"

"Silence!" cried at this moment the aged Artadi, as he showed himself at the window. "By the love which my daughter bears towards you, I will give you a further term; but do not forget that if within fifteen days you do not bring your *millares*, [6] the maiden of Artadi will be the bride of the Echejaun of Igueldo. May heaven assist you!"

"Perhaps it will be the evil one," cried the bold youth, in great wrath, "since heaven is deaf to my pleadings and cries!"

A tremendous thunder-clap was the reply to this impious exclamation, while a dart of lightning clove in twain the massive trunk of an enormous oak tree which grew close to him.

Iranzu raised his head, and, with a look of deepest contempt on his countenance, glanced up at the dark window, and began running over mountain and valley, without aim or object, roaring with rage, and invoking in one breath both heaven and hell. On turning round the brow of a hill, a-pale blue light appeared before him, and this flame flickered in an agitated manner, as though it shuddered at every movement. The young man stood still for a moment, as he gazed upon it with absorbing interest; but its pale, mysterious gleams strangely filled his soul with superstitious dread, and he turned back to avoid it. Yet the flame continued before him, and at length, annoyed at not being able to avoid or depart from it, he decided to continue his march forward; so he impetuously ran to encounter it, in order to drive. it away. But all in vain! If he advanced, the mysterious flame would flit before him; if he turned back, the flame would turn back also; yet he was unable to reach it, as it always kept at the same distance from him, fascinating his eyes, and troubling his spirit with its sinister, fantastic gleams.

"It must be my destiny!" he murmured, despondingly, and he continued to walk on, giving himself up with despairing resignation to his fate.

And they both ran and ran; the light before him floating amid the shadows in tremulous movements, Iranzu following it, taciturn and sombre. When any mountaineer approached the path Iranzu was following, and discovered the mysterious flame, he would quickly make the sign of the Cross and hasten his pace. The night was far advanced when they reached to Iciar. The flame went into the streets, and the youth still behind it. But on turning into the open space or square before the church, the light glided swiftly over the door of the temple, and after flickering for a few moments with rapid movements, it vanished among the shadows. Notwithstanding the darkness of night, the youth observed that the church door was half open, so he stepped into the porch to look within. Black thoughts of crime must have at that moment risen up in his mind, because, on drawing back from the door, his eyes were glistening with sinister fire. Overcome, or rather led by some undefinable emotion, he once again looked into the interior with eager looks; but he only discovered the shadows cast forth by the holy images, and which moved beneath the flickering gleams shed by the expiring light of the lamp. Meanwhile

116

dark thoughts assailed him each time with greater force, and he was maddened by tempting visions, and these temptations were dragging him towards the temple to manifest to his avaricious eyes the riches which were within. But he still wrestled between the voice of temptation and the voice of conscience, and he tremblingly murmured, without daring to enter, "That light is the one which is guiding me here--oh, light of my destiny! From whence does it come? Perchance from the lower regions? But no matter! If it affords me the needed *millares*, it will give me happiness!"

He vacillated for a moment; then, making a supreme effort, he leaped across the threshold, and with firm step advanced to the altar of the Lady Chapel. In those days--as at the present time--the brow of the holy image was encircled by a rich diadem of gold studded with precious stones, and from the hands pended beads of inestimable value.

On finding himself standing at the altar, Iranzu felt his knees quail under him. "Oh, if I had all these precious things!" he said, as he gazed with longing looks at the image--"oh, if I had the courage! But it is such a sacred image, and hallowed by so many miracles--who would dare to raise his wicked hand to touch its holy brow?" Nevertheless he was instinctively approaching nearer and nearer to its side, until he stood on the altar.

A gust of wind at that moment moved the curtain which veiled the sacred queen of the angels. The youth trembled, yet he continued on the altar. Suddenly throughout the wide vaulted dome of the temple resounded the prolonged echoes of a far distant discharge of guns, and then another and another, until they numbered twenty-one. [7]

It was the tender, respectful salute which from the far distant ocean some brave sailor was directing to Our Lady of Iciar, the Star of the Sea.

"What was I going to do--I, hapless man?" he murmured, as he leaped down from the altar. "Some brave one, perhaps my brother Joanes, is sending across the shades of night his homage and prayers to the Mother of God, meanwhile that my sacrilegious hand is stretched forth to wrench off her crown I No, never, never will I stain my soul with such an impious deed! It is better to die at once! Death stifles in its arms at once misery and sorrow!"

Saying this, he flung himself on his knees at the feet of the Virgin and sobbed a prayer, while two burning tears coursed down his cheeks. But these pious feelings and emotions were of short duration in a heart puffed up with pride.

The evil one whom he had invoked in his senseless despair cast a deadly shadow over his better nature, and presented before his mind and feverish imagination the image of his beloved one, her eyes streaming with tears, her heart agitated, and calling him in sad, passionate tones. And he, on the wings of love, seemed to be flying to her side, and to clasp her in his arms; but her father appeared to come to separate them, delivering her up to his hateful rival who was taking her away for ever. And in the midst of his delirium he heard distinctly ringing in his ears those hateful words of the old man--"Do not forget if within fifteen days you do not bring your *millares*, the maiden of Artadi shall be the bride of the Eche-jaun of Igueldo."

Love, jealousy, wrath, and vengeance cast flames of fire over his proud heart, a vertigo of rage took possession of his head, and, giving a leap, he stood on the altar and tore down the curtains which veiled the holy image, and, wrenching off the splendid crown which encircled its brow, he precipitately ran out of the church. On bounding over the threshold he heard almost in his very ears a frightful unearthly peal of laughter which well-nigh froze the blood in his veins, and was re-echoed in the inmost recesses of his heart like a cry of death. Maddened with terror at what he had done, he started in a wild career along the skirt of Murguizabel, without noticing that the aged *Astiya*, who, was concealed behind one of the recesses of the porch, was watching him with a look of sinister satisfaction. And he sped on and on until his chest became. contracted, and his breath failed him, and his legs tottered and bent under him. He stopped to try and recover breath for a moment, but on attempting it he thought to hear anew that terrible, awful peal of laughter, and uttering a cry of anguish, he began again to run along the broken rocks, and leaping across. torrents with senseless, fearful impetus, casting froth from out of his mouth, and darts of fire from his eyes.

The night was dark, very dark. The hurricane was breaking over the land, the wind whistled among the aged oaks, and their dry branches, moving under the impulses of the wind, appeared to be ill-omened phantoms, that were putting forth their weird arms towards the guilty youth, whilst the shadows cast by the bushes, the broken rocks, and the briery hedges which waved around him, conjured up in his terrified imagination legions of devils that sprang up on every side as he trod the ground.

And thus he walked on for one hour, and two--and six--without stopping once, without lessening his pace, scarcely daring to breathe, until at the dawn of the new day he ceased to hear that fiendish laughter, as the shades of night disappeared, and the wind became calmed down. Exhausted and breathless, he stopped at the foot of a chestnut tree to rest awhile; but, wishing first to know whereabouts he was, he climbed the tree to reconnoitre the ground.

"How much I must have walked!" he murmured while he climbed up. "I must be far, very far away!"

It was the hour when the day wrestles to open a way amid the shadows, piercing through and pouring on all sides a dim misty light which alters every object.

"I can distinguish nothing," he said, fixing his eyes with yearning looks towards the east, where the horizon was beginning to be tinged with the soft light of dawn.

All at once the sun, rending the mists and fogs with powerful impulse, inundated with torrents of light a magnificent temple which rose up dark and sombre at the foot of the white cliffs of Andutz. On recognizing it, the hapless youth felt his heart chilled within him with horror, and a cold perspiration overspread his pale, weary forehead. The building which appeared before his astonished gaze was the Church of Our Lady of Iciar, from which he had been unable to depart more than a thousand yards during seven hours of frenzied speed.

Believing that he was the victim of some nightmare, he closed his eyes to shut out this awe-inspiring vision, and on opening them again he saw on all sides the forms of armed men who were approaching, seeking something among the briers and bushes. No doubt the sacrilegious robbery had been discovered, and these men had come seeking the thief. Convinced at that moment of the terrible reality, he bent down his head in deep despondency and terror. Meanwhile the men were approaching, closely following his footprints step by step. Iranzu, perceiving this, wished to leap down, but the stolen jewels weighed him down terribly, and he was unable to move a foot as though he were nailed to the tree. Bewailing his powerlessness, he wished at least to cast the jewels from him in order to conceal his crime, but, on putting his hand to his breast where he had hidden them, he felt his fingers become charred at the contact. In this terrible anguish he made a last and desperate attempt to tear the cloth off his tunic; but it was in vain that he employed all his strength. The fragile cloth resisted his efforts as though it had been made of woven steel.

By this time the men had discovered him, and were coming quickly to the tree, tracing a circle in order to prevent his escape. Oh, then did he curse his ill-fated love, his existence, and his crime; and then, unclasping the belt he wore, he made a noose with it, and in despair hung himself from one of the branches.

When his pursuers reached him, they found him in the last throes of death, and he only lived long enough to be able to recount the sad circumstances of his sacrilegious attempt.

Since that epoch the brow of the mountain on which this event took place is known throughout the district by the name of *Hurca-Mendi*--that is to say, the mountain of the gibbet. On the left extends the ancient roadway which leads from Iciar to the sea; and if any one desirous of investigating these legends advances by that side towards the deserted slopes of Arbill, the shepherds who tend the flocks there will show him the spot on which the unhappy, ill-advised youth put an end to his days, adding that during the darksome nights of winter there are heard the doleful sighs of his spirit as it wanders among the woods.

[1] *Hurca-Mendi.* See Glossary.
[2] *Gara-paita.* See Glossary.
[3] *Astiya.* See Glossary.
[4] *A tile, a tree,* &c. See Glossary.
[5] *Aitz-belz.* See Glossary.
[6] *Millares.* See Glossary.
[7] *Twenty-one.* See Glossary.

Glossary

A tile, a tree, and a coat of mail. By the *fueros* of Biscay the eldest son inherited all the property, leaving to the other brothers only the mail as a knight: a tree, to signify, no doubt, the deeply-rooted family stock of nobility, and a tile, as representing the family house.

Achular. A mountain of Guipuzcoa, close to Andoain. There is another of the same name in the valley of Lerin, in Navarre.

Aitz-belz. The black cliff. By this name is known a mountain of Mendaro, in which there is a chasm so deep that the people believe that it ends in the bottomless pit of hell.

Aitzgorri. Mountain of Guipuzcoa: a continuation of Aloña. It rises 1·800 metres above the level of the sea.

Aloña. A mountain of Guipuzcoa, at whose southerly base is situated the magnificent town of Oñate, where, for a long time during the seven years' civil war, the Infante Don Carlos de Bourbon, uncle of Isabella II., held his court.

Amboto. A very high cliff situated on the frontiers of Guipuzcoa, Alava, and Biscay.

Aquelarre. A word composed of *larre*, pasture land, and *Aquerra*, buck goat; hence the word *Aquelarre* signifies the *pasture land of the goat*. It is well known that this animal figures in all the conventicles of witches as representing the Evil One.

Aránzan, zu. Literally, "You, in a thorn?"

Aránzanzu, Convent of. Situated on the south-west of the Monte Aloña. The convent was under the invocation of Our Lady of Aránzanzu, and was inhabited by the friars of the Order of St. Francis. The situation of this convent was very remarkable. It was cast, so to say, on the highest point and most rugged and bare of the mountain, on the height of a steep declivity, and from this may be inferred the daring and solidity of that capricious construction, Throughout the three Basque provinces the holy image of Our Lady of Aránzanzu was very famous, and the devotion of the people for it, even in our days, very general. During the month of May it is visited by numerous pilgrimages, and nothing more fantastic can be imagined than the effect produced by the glare of the fires at night, which are lit by the multitudes encamped on the mountain, as they are unable to find accommodation for all in the spacious inns close to the convent, and to listen to the echoes of the magnificent organ, instrumental orchestra, and large choir of voices, as they celebrate the praises of the Virgin and intoned the prayers. The convent was only visible at a distance of about fifty metres. I am sorry to add that this singular construction was set fire to by order of General Rodil, during the civil war against Don Carlos--a deed of barbarism which will always merit repre-hension and condemnation.

Arguiduna. Fatuous fire, or Will-o'-the-Wisp.

Articuza. Palace and stronghold close to the shores of that name. They are situated in the centre of the mountains of Goizueta, ten kilometres from the town, and surrounded by dense woods and forests.

Asté, *Sem*, *Nestos*, and *Heas*. Mountainous and deserted places in the centre of the Pyrenees.

Astiya. A Basque word which is equal to "Witch," or one professing to pos-sess the art of divination, or of casting spells or charms over people.

Bardena Real. A deserted and plain cut through by rocks and broken boul-ders, extending from the junction of the rivers Ebro and Aragon to within two kilometres beyond the frontier of the ancient kingdom of Aragon, a dis-tance comprehending many kilometres.

Basso-jaun. Literally translated it signifies the *Lord of the Woods*. The su-perstitious imagination of the Basques depicts him as a horrible monster in human form, covered with hair, and having nails long and hard as those of a wild boar. It is supposed to reside in the deepest part of the woods, and occa-sionally it appears at the mouths of caverns and in mountain torrents. Very curious are the details which are given concerning this popular belief, by M. Michel, in his work entitled "Le Pais Basque."

Begoña. The church of Begoña stands in the neighbourhood of Bilbao, on the eminence of Artagan, which overlooks the town.. It is one of the most re-nowned temples of these provinces. The present temple was constructed at the commencement of the sixteenth century, but from time immemorial the Virgin Mary has been venerated there under the invocation of Santa Maria de Begoña. Tradition tells us that its miraculous image appeared on that spot, and, on endeavouring to erect a church on the summit of the mountain, they went in procession to conduct the image to the place where they intended to build the edifice, but they heard a mysterious voice which said, *Bego-oña* ("Keep still"), and from this voice was the name given of Begoña.

Benzozia. The Venus of chaste love of the primitive Basques.

Berderiz. A mountain situated at two kilometres from the town of Irurita, in the valley of Baztan.

Bertizarana, Baztan, Aezcoa, Erro, RONCAL. Valleys of Navarre, on the fron-tiers of France. The three first are narrow and surrounded by very high mountains.

Cadagüa. This is the most powerful river of Biscay, after that of Ibaizabal. It has its origin in the highest part of the vale of Mena, which anciently be-longed to Biscay, and at the present day to Burgos. It flows along the En-cartaciones of Biscay, and joins the Ibaizabal about a league below Bilbao.

Cahella, Belaya, Ahaide. High and very luxuriant mountains, close to the valley of Roncal, in Navarre.

Canigou. A high and inaccessible mountain of the French Pyrenees; part corresponds to Spain.

Cannas. A celebrated battle gained by Hannibal against the Romans. A vanguard of the Carthaginian army which decided the victory was composed of Basque auxiliaries.

Cantabrians. A people of Hispana Tarraconeza, between the Pyrenees and the Ocean, inhabiting Navarre, Biscay, Alava, and Guipuzcoa.

Capusay. A sort of dalmatic of very thick cloth furnished with a hood.

Clemencia Isaura. A lady of rank descended from the nobles of Tolosa. She lived in the fifteenth century. It was she who revived in that city the famous floral games, which had fallen into disuse for more than a century, and she left at her death, in 1513, a considerable sum for defraying the expenses of these poetic tournaments.

Covadonga, Navas, and *Salado.* Three famous sanguinary battles, in which the Moors were routed: in these the Basque legions took an active part.

Dalmatic. A very rich robe embroidered with gold spangles, worn over tunics of white wool on great festivals by the ancient Euscaros in olden times. This dalmatic was used as a sign of authority. The shape of this robe is exactly as the vestments worn during High Mass by the officiating deacon and subdeacon, with the sole difference that the dalmatic has a hood. The "capusay" of the shepherds and country people of our time, worn in the Basque country, is an exact copy of that very ancient robe.

Durango. Principal town of Biscay.

Echeco-jauna. The head of the family, proprietor, &c.

Elzupel, Otsobide, Hernio, Aitzgorri. Mountains. The two first belong to Navarre, and the third to Guipuzcoa.

Embrun. A cistern or reservoir in Palestine, much renowned in the time of the Crusaders.

Eskaldunac. Some authors write it *Escualdunac* (from *escua*, hand, *alde*, right, *dunac*, those who have), a name which the Biscayans, or Basque people, give to themselves. In their dialect they call themselves Euskarians. This dialect, the wise Humboldt considered, was the most remarkable language of all he was acquainted with.

Esquiroz. A mountain situated in Navarre, on the confines of Bardena Real.

Euscuara, or *Euscara.* The name given by the Basque to those who speak it. See Essay on the Basque Language, by M. Julien Vinson, in "Basque Legends," by the Rev. Wentworth Webster.

Five Towns of Aragon. A group composed of the towns of *Sos*, Sadava, *Uncastillo*, *Tauste*, and *Egea*--all situated on the frontiers of Aragon and Navarre, to the extreme of the Pyrenees.

Gara-paita. The collecting of the brake fern. This is a rustic agricultural work in which all the neighbours and relatives join the landowner. It generally lasts several days, and each evening, when the day's labour is over, the young people amuse themselves with music, dancing, and love-making; while the old people spend the time in games, or recounting tales or ballads. In this way they convert what would otherwise be a laborious work into a regular country feast.

Gorbea. A mountain of Alava, which overlooks the plain upon which stands the city of Vitoria.

Guernica, *Arriaga*, and *Guerekiz*. The three camps where in ancient times were gathered together the *bill-zaars*, or meetings of the ancients. The first was in Alava, the second in Biscay, and the third in Guipuzcoa.

Guernicáco Arbola. The Tree of Guernica. This is one of the patriotic songs dedicated to the tree of Basque liberties, which is close to the town of Guernica, in Biscay. The actual tree is nearly a century old, since it was only thirty years old when its predecessor fell down from old age in 1811, and that one numbered more than three hundred years when it fell. Its trunk, says Iturriza, at the end of last century, was fifteen feet in circumference. The origin of this symbolical tree of the Basque liberties dates back to the origin of the Biscayan society. The statute tree is perpetuated like the Euskarian family, and is succeeded by its scions. The general *juntas* are materially inaugurated under the tree, and are continued in the juridical church of Santa Maria la Antigua, placed also materially under the shadow of the statute oak. The actual tree is robust and beautiful, notwithstanding that it was greatly injured in 1830 or 1850 by the erection of the building intended for the general archive of the province. The tree which is to substitute the present one was planted a few years ago. Poetry and oratory have many times enthusiastically saluted the Tree of Guernica. The philosopher of Geneva sent it his blessing. Tallien saluted it in the midst of the French Convention, and many Spanish poets have written charming odes to the tree. The lords of Biscay took their oaths seated on a stone bench placed at the foot of the tree. It was on that spot that the Catholic Kings Ferdinand and Isabella sat, as also other monarchs. There is a patriotic song dedicated to the tree, and runs as follows

El Arbol de Guernica
es bendecido
Y entre los vascongados
Amado de todos.
Propaga y estiende
tu fruto por el mundo
Nosotros te adoramos
Arbol Santo!
Ha cerca de mil años.
Segun se dice
que Dios plantó,
El Arbol de Guernica.
Permanece erguido
porque si ahora
caes,
Somos completamente perdidos.
No caerás
Arbol amado

123

Si procede bien
el Congreso de Vizcaya.
Las cuatro tomaremos
parte en tu sosten
para que viva en paz
el pueblo vascongado.
Viva eternamente,
Y para pedirselo al Señor
Prosternémonos todos
Al punto de rodillas:
Y cuando de todo corazon
hayamos orado
El Arbol viverá
en lo presente y lo porvenir.

Guesalza. A cave of great depth and extension, full of crystals. It is situated near the Mondragon, in Guipuzcoa.

Holy Oak, The. This is the Tree of Guernica, the symbol of the Basque liberties.

Hurca-Mendi. A Basque word composed of *hurca*, gibbet, and *mendia*, mountain. This is the name of the place in which occurred the event referred to in the tale. In past times it was called *Hurca-mendi-mendia*, that is to say, the mountain of the gibbet, but at the present day the last word is suppressed, and is only known as in the title of the tradition.

Ibaizabal. A word equivalent to "Wide River." It is the name given by the Basques to the river Nervion, which proceeds from the mountains Durango and Orduña, and, passing Bilbao, empties itself into the sea at Portugalete, or, rather, between Santurce and Algorta, which stand to the right and left of the bar.

Irati. One of the principal mountains of Navarre. It is covered by dense woods, in which are found lynx, bears, wolves, and all kinds of large game. The circumference of the base of this mountain measures about fifty kilometres. One part corresponds to France, and the rest to Navarre.

Irrinzi. The shout, or call of war.

Iturrioz. Fonte fria. The cold fountain.

Izalzu. A village situated five kilometres from Ochagabia, in the valley of Aezcoa, in Navarre.

Izaspi. An ancient place of Navarre.

Jaizquibel. A mountain which rises parallel to the Cantabrian Sea from the Port of Passagens to that of Fuenterrabia. At its extreme north there stood anciently the promontory of Olearso, in our days the Cape of Higuer.

Jauregui (Gaspar). Field-marshal in the service of the Queen D. Isabella II. He was a native of Villa-real, of Guipuzcoa. He had been a shepherd, and during the war against Napoleon was an untiring guerilla chief.

Kuruceta. A mountain situated in Guipuzcoa and Navarre, upon which some hundreds of Basque prisoners were crucified during the wars against the Romans.

Kurucificatuaren Canta. (*The Chant of the Crucified*.) During the long and sanguinary war sustained by the Romans against the inhabitants of the Basque mountains, the prisoners who fell into the power of the Romans were crucified on the summit of the mountains, with the object of inspiring the dwellers with terror. The heroic Basques intoned, while on the cross, a chant of triumph and death, and also insulted their enemies, who witnessed with feelings of awe such manifestations of courage and lofty independence of spirit.

Lamia. The Basque water-nymph, or mermaid.

Lara. A young bard and Basque chief of the period when the wars were raging against the Empire of Rome. The poet Silio Italico, in the sixteenth book of his Epic Poem, assigned a whole page to describe the personal combat of Lara against Scipio, in which the Basque chief lost his right hand.

Lecayo. A cry of joy which is used as a signal.

Left hand of a child, The. It was a general belief among the mountain dwellers of the Basque provinces that the left hand of a child, if severed during sleep, and wrapped round with curls of its own hair, became a valuable amulet, which would deliver them of every kind of danger, and with it philters of different properties could also be made. There yet exists some among the rude inhabitants of the mountains of Roncal who foster this superstitious belief, although examples are unknown of this cruel mutilation ever having been effected, unless by the artifice of *gipsies*, *agotes*, or Jews in very remote ages, as there still exists evidence of severe provisions having been adopted against these barbarians. It was also a popular belief that the blood of children was useful for invigorating the weak bodies of women.

Maitagarri. Among the Basque people this is a fairy, or hade, which inhabits the lakes, and corresponds to the "Peri," or the Genius of the Persians. According to the legend, or popular tradition, this fairy, or hade, fell in love with a shepherd called Luzaide, and she took him to the summit of Ahuñemendi, where she had her palace made of crystal. This legend evidently forms the basis of the narrative which the author gives in this chapter.

Millares. By this name was anciently designated the amount of real property levied by the *fueros* as a tax, but later on this term comprehended all wealth derived from inheritance, dowries, or other bequests.

Montlig and *Astarac*. Deserted places of the French Pyrenees.

Nive. A French river, which springs on the declivity to the north of the Western Pyrenees, and joins the river Adour in Bayonne, and jointly flows into the Cantabrian Ocean.

Novempopulania. During the epoch of the domination of the Romans, this district extended from the Cantabrian Ocean to the margin of the river Garrona, and from the first slope of the French Pyrenees to the margin of the above-said river and its mouth into the sea, forming an acute angle.

Odolaga. A mountain which, forming a cordillera, separates the valleys of Baztan and Ulzama. It is covered with woods.

Orbara. A precipitous defile of the valley of Aezcoa, in Navarre.

Otsondo. A mountain on the frontiers of France, near the Urdax, in Navarre.

Padura. A parochial district of Biscay. It was here that the natives completely routed the army of Ordoño the Wicked. At the present day this spot is known under the name of *Arrigorriaga* (Red stones), an appellation given to it, as tradition informs us, on account of the great quantity of blood which was spilt on the stones and imparted a red colour to them.

Quidaria. Chieftain.

Regil. The ancient Errazill. A town close to Tolosa, of Guipuzcoa. Its inhabitants routed the Romans in the time of Augustus.

Sumbilla. A lovely, picturesque town of Navarre, situated in the valley of Lerin, on the straight line with Vidassoa, about thirty-five kilometres from Pamplona.

Tejo. A very common tree of the Basque mountains, the sap of which is poisonous. The Cantabrians used to poison themselves with this sap rather than surrender to the enemy. From this word Tejo was derived the name of *Toxicum*, or *tosigo*, which, later on, was applied to all descriptions of poison. Thousands of persons, principally among the aged men and women, took this poison, according to Roman historians, in Medulia and in the Hirnio, to save themselves from slavery and chains.

Tolosa. The capital of the province of Guipuzcoa.

Twenty-one. It was a custom of immemorial origin among the Basque people for ships to fire twenty-one guns on sighting the church of Our Lady of Iciar, venerated under this invocation as the especial protectress of mariners.

Zulogaraya, *Izotzce*, and *Asarosta*. Defiles of the French Pyrenees, which have their commencement in Spanish territory.

Zumalacarregui (Thomas). A native of Ormaiztegui, in Guipuzcoa. He was general-in-chief of the army of Don Carlos. He died from the effects of a wound received in the first siege of Bilbao, in 1835. He was one of the best Spanish generals of this century.